SON OF TH

Son of the Furrows

Jane Sleight is an author fascinated by relationships in the modern age. Her first books were the **Tales of a Modern Woman** novel trilogy and the novel **Sasha** - a tale of womanhood in the 21st century. Her first novella was **Walking Back Toward Myself** - a tale of self-rediscovery set in Cumbria. **Like Father, Like Son** and **The Secret of Contentment** are both romantic intrigues exploring reasons why people hide secrets from their partners. She has also written **Crumbs from the Bread of Life**, a collection of contemporary poetry and short stories, and a three-act play called **Womanipulation**, that examines the nature of friendship between women. Her latest novel **Faking It** was published in 2023.

You can find updates from Jane on Twitter **@janesleight**, on Facebook **@JaneSleightAuthor** and at her website **janesleight.com**.

By Jane Sleight

Novels

The *Tales of a Modern Woman* series

Part 1 - Teen Rebel to Woman

Part 2 – From Woman to Wife

Part 3 – Happy Ever After?

Standalone Novels

Sasha

Faking It

Novellas

Walking Back Toward Myself

Like Father, Like Son

The Secret of Contentment

Short Stories and Poetry

Crumbs from the Bread of Life

Jane Sleight

Son of the Furrows

A contemporary novella with a supernatural twist

Jane Sleight Publishing

JANE SLEIGHT

First published 2023 by Jane Sleight Publishing

Copyright © Jane Sleight 2023

All rights reserved. No part of this publication may be reproduced, stored in a retrieval system or transmitted in any form or by any means, electronic, mechanical, photocopying, recording or otherwise, without written permission of the author.

Acknowledgements

Thank you to my amazing husband for not complaining about the amount of time I spend scribbling in notebooks.

Thank you to my beta readers, Amanda, Jain and Gary, as well as the members of Rushmoor Writers, whose responses and invaluable advice gave me the confidence to share Farlan and Lucy with the world.

JANE SLEIGHT

Chapter 1

A sliver of moon was shining brightly enough for me to see the garden out of the bedroom window. There was a fox digging in our vegetable bed, in search of worms, I assumed, as there was nothing left of our sorry attempts to grow anything worth eating. I climbed back into bed as gently as I could. Waking James at 3:30am was guaranteed to cause an unwelcome rant.

'Look at that.' James shook me by the shoulder and I faked a yawn, even though I'd been lying awake since the fox's visit and had heard James get out of bed.

'What?' I tried to sound sleepy.

'Bloody mess in the garden. I thought it was next door's scabby tabby but I've been out there and the smell is gross. Has to be a fox. We need some kind of deterrent.'

'What time is it?' I asked, even though I knew.

'6:25am. Almost time to get up.' He looked sideways at me as I flung off the duvet. 'God, your thighs are enormous. Don't you think it's time you did some exercise, Lucy?'

My jaw hardened and my teeth ground against each other. 'Sod you. Have you seen your paunch in the mirror lately?'

He sucked in his stomach. It didn't make much difference. He still looked decidedly middle-aged. That was the price I paid for living with someone ten years my senior. James was sensible and risk-averse, which countered my occasionally foolish tendencies but…but what, Lucy? I asked myself.

'I can still fit into thirty-eight-inch-waist trousers.' He tried to keep his stomach muscles clenched.

I could have been cruel and pointed out that the overhang of his belly was much bigger than that but I bit it back. I gave a shrug and got up.

I went downstairs when I woke up the next night, disturbed again by a noise outside. I watched through the patio doors as Mr Fox made his balletic entrance up and along our garden wall before jumping down into the vegetable bed. Of course, it might be Mrs Fox. I wondered if Mr Fox was back in the family lair, snoring like James. The fox looked up, staring as though it could hear my thoughts. It was unnerving, yet I couldn't fight the urge to go out and see it. I kept eye contact with it as much as I could while I unlocked the door and tiptoed across the patio and onto the gravelled area where our three vegetable beds stood. I got to within touching distance of the beautiful creature and our eyes locked together.

I swear it smiled at me before it disappeared. Disappeared before my eyes. I gasped and the cold air hit my throat. What the hell happened? In the fox's place lay a large, old-fashioned key, with a brown cardboard label. I picked it up. There was a single, handwritten word. Fetlar. Fetlar? What the hell was Fetlar? Looked like an anagram of something.

SON OF THE FURROWS

I crept back into the house, clutching the key while my brain tried to rearrange the letters of this word I'd not heard before. Fartle? Lafter? Falter? At least that was a word. I gave up and went, as quietly as I could, into the bedroom to retrieve my phone. I searched for Fetlar and found it was one of the Shetland Islands. About as far away from Croydon as you could get without a passport. I went into the study and hid the key in the drawer that had become the place where everything that might be useful one day gets dumped. Even if James looked in there, he'd never find it.

I went into the spare bedroom. It had become my temporary workspace, now that lockdown-enforced working from home had become a permanent thing. I closed the door and switched on my laptop, waiting for it to whirr into life, feeling a bubble of excitement in my stomach. I had some holiday leave to take. Why not go to Fetlar?

A couple of hours later, I stretched and yawned. I'd discovered a lot about Fetlar and how to get there. It was not a quick journey. I needed two flights, a hire car to drive across the islands and a couple of ferry crossings but it would be an adventure. All I had to do was book some leave from work and I'd be able to go. I dozed on the spare bed till it was almost time to get up. James didn't appear to have noticed my absence from our bed. He would have mentioned it when he got up if he had, as a complaint, probably. He got ready for work, moaning about something. I was too busy thinking about Fetlar to listen to exactly what had irked him that morning. There was always something. He left for the station at

7:15am with barely a goodbye, but he was pre-occupied with his latest work project, so I gave him the benefit of the doubt.

I thought properly about what had happened once I was alone in the house. I mean, it was crazy, I said out loud, as I made myself a cup of tea before I started work. A key magically appearing? Maybe it had been there all the time and the fox had run off really quickly. Whatever it was, I had a perfect opportunity to follow the trail. I'd been wondering what to do with the rest of my leave. James had used up most of his holiday on a European football tour with his mates from the pub, so I'd tell him I was going on a mindfulness course. He'd never know that wasn't true, that I was randomly travelling to the end of the country in search of a door to match the key that had turned up magically in our garden, brought there by a disappearing fox. If I'd told him that, he'd have had me sectioned.

I must have gone to the study drawer and checked the key was still there a dozen times already that morning, every time thinking it would be gone, which would prove I was definitely going mad. But it was still there, a physical symbol of the happening in the night and a confirmation of the decision I'd made to go on this journey. I examined it more carefully. The iron key was about 10cm long with a few rust spots and it seemed genuinely old. The label was old-fashioned, the sort of cardboard tag that Paddington Bear wore around his neck in picture books. The word Fetlar was written in ink, proper ink, not biro. The writing was smart but it wasn't calligraphy, just large, neat, plain letters. Nothing about the key or the label helped me make sense of what had happened.

SON OF THE FURROWS

I sent a message to Pete, my boss, as soon as he logged on that morning, saying that something had come up and I needed some time away. He was fine with it. I was expecting an inquisition but in truth, he wasn't interested. James and he were old friends and they were cut from the same cloth. Not big on detail or curious about other people.

I went ahead and booked two flights – one to Edinburgh from London and one from Edinburgh to Sumburgh. I booked a hire car from Sumburgh airport as well as the ferry tickets. The first boat would take me from the north of the main island of Shetland to Yell and the second from Yell to Fetlar. It would take a couple of days to reach my destination but it didn't matter. I was a woman on a mission, albeit one without any clear purpose.

I told James I was going away when he got home from work that night. He was entirely accepting of my short notice trip. He agreed to drop me off at the airport and didn't ask any questions about what I'd be doing and where exactly I was going. I wasn't sure if it was a lack of curiosity on his part or an absence of caring. Either way, I was delighted there was no-one standing in the way of my spontaneous journey. I rarely made rash decisions but when I did, I followed through wholeheartedly.

I packed my bag that night and thought about ringing my bestie, Ali, to tell her about my trip. She hadn't been in touch for ages when I thought about it. I looked back over our exchanged messages. We'd had dinner a little over a year ago. As I scrolled through WhatsApp, I could see that we'd have three conversations since that dinner. That had been the night she'd told me she was pregnant. I'd been the instigator of all of the messages since then but she was a mum now and from the social media updates she'd posted previously, she'd had a hard time with morning sickness and that diabetes you get in pregnancy. I'd seen her post pictures on Instagram of the boy she'd been blessed with a few months back. I'd sent a baby box with the cutest Winnie the Pooh-themed gifts and tried to visit but she'd put me off, citing tiredness. "Let me know when you're up for a visit" had been my last message to her. She must be busy with her family life and I couldn't blame her for that. She probably wouldn't understand my desire to get away. She'd see it as an indulgence and say how lucky I was that I had enough money and time to be able to take the trip.

I dropped her a message, asking how everything was going and she sent back a picture of a sleeping baby. I responded with a heart emoji and went back to my packing.

Chapter 2

I hugged myself with excitement as I left James moaning about the drop-off charge at Heathrow. Google provided me with plenty of information about the Shetland Islands as I travelled. It sounded a fascinating place with castle ruins, Iron Age villages, Norse settlements and nature reserves spread across the various islands. Fetlar itself was small, though it was the fourth-largest of the islands. Despite its size, it still had some interesting attractions for me to explore. It was the sort of place I'd have gone for a break, before I met James. I liked quirky destinations. All he wanted was sunshine and beer. I got through a lot of books on our holidays, sitting on a sunbed with my pale skin plastered in factor 50 sunblock. I scanned every web page I could find but there was no mention of foxes in the descriptions of the Shetland flora and fauna. Maybe it was going to be a wasted journey. Thinking about it though, there didn't need to be any foxes there. Not now I had the key. All I had to do was find the keyhole it opened. Fetlar wasn't that big an island. How hard could it be? That was assuming I didn't get arrested for breaking and entering in the process.

I overnighted in a cheap hotel near Edinburgh Airport, glad I'd brought my warmest clothing as the heating was either on the blink or not on at all. Maybe they were used to the cold and it was only Southern softies like me that needed heating at this time of year.

The next day, I took the second flight and picked up a hire car, driving along a winding road northward onto a bumpy ferry, followed by another drive and a second boat trip, which was a lot rougher than the first. As I finally drove off the boat and onto Fetlar, I forgot the effort and discomfort of getting there and felt I'd burst with the excitement of having my first solo adventure in a long time. I pulled up at the first passing place so I could get out and smell the air. It was a family ritual. My father made us all do it as soon as we arrived in a foreign country. "Really smell it, Lucy. Take a deep breath. Warmer air smells different, doesn't it?" Sometimes there'd be the smell of herbs, trees or even dust. He was like a wine connoisseur but for air. I lost myself in the moment and as it passed, I felt alive as I stood there, awakened, thrilled at the thought of what lay ahead, even though I had no idea what that would be. It had been a surprise to me how keen I was to escape my Croydon existence. It was a life I'd had for the last four-and-a-half years and I was seemingly content with it. I dismissed the thought, shaking my head to dislodge it. There'd be plenty of time for thinking while I was here.

It was already starting to get dark as I headed to my accommodation. I followed the directions, glad I'd printed them out, as my phone had stopped picking up a reasonable signal. My destination was a smart, white house and I was glad there were lights on inside.

'You must be Lucy. I'm Lorna,' the lady at the door said.

'Hi. It's great to be here,' I said.

She showed me around, pointing me at the information folder about the house. She told me twice that it contained the Wi-Fi code, as though internet access was the most important facility on offer. Maybe to some people it was, but I was happy to get away from technology. I asked if anyone else was booked in after me and Lorna said there were no bookings for the rest of the month. I'd only paid for three days, in case it all turned out to be a huge waste of time. Lorna wished me a happy holiday and left me to settle in.

I focused on what would be my home for the next few days. The key to the house was a modern Yale lock and the outbuildings had smart padlocks on their entrances, but I didn't expect it to be that easy to find where the mysterious key fitted. The house itself was well-equipped, warm and private. The larger house across from it was empty, Lorna had said, because the birdwatchers who frequented the island were scarce at this time of year. The solitude both gladdened and unsettled me, after the busyness of Croydon. I took a nip from a miniature whisky bottle that had been left in the kitchen, shuddering because I didn't like the taste. I turned off the light to watch the last of the sunset and sat on a time-bleached blue sofa, listening to the wind, enjoying the sense of peace as I let my thoughts swirl around my brain like leaves on a breeze.

I woke with a start. I was still on the blue sofa but was lying down. It was dark, so I took my phone from my coat pocket to see the time. Just after 3am. I turned on the phone's torch so I could get to the window without tripping over and look out into the night. There was no light anywhere in the vicinity so I switched mine off to let my eyes grow accustomed. After a while, I began to make out vague shapes. As I scanned the view, there was a flash, low to the ground. A pair of eyes shone out of the gloom and were staring back at me. It was the fox. Well, it was a fox, not the fox. Who was

I kidding? The way its eyes were trained on me like a sniper's sight, it had to be the same beast I'd seen in my garden. It stared at me for an age then disappeared. I turned the phone torch back on and dashed outside to where I'd seen the fox but there was nothing. No key, no sign, no instructions. But what did I expect? A treasure map?

I went back into the house, locking the door behind me and got into bed, pulling off my boots and coat but not bothering to undress. The fox's gaze appeared in my mind's eye as I tried to sleep. It wasn't frightening, just a little unnerving. Come on, Lucy, I said to myself. Given what had happened in Croydon, and the fact that I'd temporarily abandoned my normal life to come here because of it, I should have been relieved my vulpine visitor had returned to me. Even if I still hadn't a clue what else to do. In the morning, I'd see if I could find a home for the key.

Chapter 3

It was grey and drizzly when I woke up. I was starving and the only food I had with me was an old Werther's Original that was stuck to the inside of my jacket pocket. I decided to go to the local shop, which I was sure I'd read was open daily at this time of year. I got dressed and put on my waterproof jacket. It was less than half a mile but I decided to drive, buy some food then go exploring. I picked up the keys to the hire car as well as the magic key. I didn't want to leave that behind.

It was 9:30am but the grey weather was robbing the sky of light when I ventured outside. The clouds were dashing overhead. The wind was fresh against my face and there was a smell of damp earth in the air.

I started the car. It was a novelty to be driving. My Croydon life was 99% public transport. I slid the car into Drive and went the short distance to Houbie. The shop looked disappointingly quiet when I pulled up. The sign on the door said it didn't open till 11am, so I got back in the car and continued my journey, going past a sign for the now-disused airport, a leather works and on to a place called Brough Lodge.

I got out of the car. It was raining properly now. I pulled my hood up and took in the view of the lodge. It looked like a work in progress. I remembered reading something about it when I'd been researching the island. The website had said it was watertight and windtight but needed money to be refurbished. I wandered around all the buildings, checking every door to see if any of them looked as though they might open with the key I had in my pocket. I circled the area twice, and went up to the door of the lodge's Astronomy Tower. Finding no equivalent of Cinderella's foot, I got in the car and drove back to the house as it still wasn't time for the shop to open.

As I sat on the sofa, I wondered what I'd do when I found the door that could be opened with the magical key. Suppose there was a nutter lurking inside. Would I disappear without trace? No-one knew where I was. Well, that wasn't true. My bank transactions were a direct trail to me. Any policeman worth their salt could find me in less than an hour, though James wouldn't raise an alarm, thinking I was out of contact by choice. Lorna would, though, if I wasn't at the house at the end of my stay. Unless she was the nutter. I laughed at myself. I'd been blessed, or was it cursed, with an over-active imagination since childhood.

By 10:45am, a flicker of sunshine had broken through the cloud, so I decided to walk to the shop. I went in as it opened and optimistically picked up a basket after shouting hello in the general direction of the till. Given how remote the island was, I was surprised at what the shop had to offer. It was hard to know what to buy, given I had no idea how long I'd be staying, so I picked up bread, cheese and fruit as well as milk and cereal. And wine. There had to be wine.

I toyed with the idea of eating in the small café that was part of the shop complex but decided to save that treat till later in my visit.

I went back to the house and ate a big bowl of some overly-sweet cereal that must have been designed to rot children's teeth, and idly read the House Information folder that Lorna had pointed out to me.

A ping on my phone signalled an email arriving. My sister had responded to my message. I'd told her about my unexpected holiday and her reply was "Fine. Enjoy". That was typical. She didn't give a shit about me since she'd moved to Stockholm to live with her latest boyfriend. She'd given up caring about me long before then, but I was fine with that. Sarah was twelve years older than me and we'd never bonded as siblings. When our parents died, I knew that signalled the end of our faux sisterly relationship. I think she found me boring but I was OK with that, because I didn't value her opinion. I wondered why I'd bothered to get in touch with her. It said more about the significance of the trip than of her.

I looked out of the window at the light and the sea and the naked beauty of the location and wondered what to do. I'd come all this way. I was 841 miles from home, all because a fox had appeared in my garden, left a magic key and vanished.

I sat in silence for a few minutes, letting my mind randomly drift. It was surprisingly restful, doing nothing. I thought about calling James, but I'd told him I'd be switching my phone off for the course and he'd been happy with that. I suspect he was relieved I wasn't going to be calling him each day to tell him about the things I'd learned on the course he thought I was on. "That happy-clappy shit", he'd called it. It was Saturday, so he'd be having a lie-in before going to the pub with his mates to watch the football, so there was no point in ringing. I asked myself why I missed him at all and felt guilty because I didn't.

Deciding I might as well enjoy the island, I set off and walked in the opposite direction from Brough Lodge. The weather was OK and I enjoyed stretching my legs for a proper walk. The road took me to a place called Funzie but the road became a track and stopped after a while, so I tried to navigate my way around the top of the island, figuring if I kept the sea on my right, I would eventually end up at the ferry terminal where I'd arrived the day before and could follow the road back.

The sky began to darken and I was glad I'd worn my waterproof jacket. I pulled the hood up as it started to rain and the visibility reduced. I couldn't believe how quickly the weather and the atmosphere had changed. I put my hand in my jacket pocket, feeling to make sure the key was still there. I kept on with determination, sure I would see the ferry soon.

But then the fox appeared. It came close to me and looked up at me, fixing my eyes with his. Once it was sure it had my attention, it turned and walked slowly inland. Figuring I'd nothing to lose, I followed. The mist continued to curl around me and the light levels were low so I lost all sense of direction. The fox waited for me to catch up then began trotting as the drizzle came down harder. Wiping the rain from my face, I lost sight of him. Looking around, with no clue where I was, I squinted at what looked like a building in the distance. I half-ran towards it. It was a single-storey stone cottage. There were dark curtains at the windows and no sign of life. I walked around the side and spotted a door.

Chapter 4

'Hello. Welcome to the retreat.'

I shook with surprise at the deep, male voice that came out of nowhere.

'Sorry, I didn't mean to startle you. Let's go in out of the rain,' the voice said.

A tall, thickset, bearded man moved from behind me to the door. I followed him in and was glad of the blast of warmth that greeted me from the fire at the opposite end of the room. There was a strong smell of peaty smoke and it reminded me of the whisky James liked to drink. I noticed the man put a key onto the small table by the entrance. It looked like the one I'd been carrying, though when I put my hand in my pocket, the key was gone. I checked the other pocket. I must have dropped it somewhere on my walk.

A woman with long, lustrous, chestnut hair, who looked about my age, appeared from somewhere beyond the fireplace. 'I'm packed and ready to go,' she said to the man.

He nodded. 'Let's have a drink before I take you to the ferry.' He turned to me. 'Jenna's been staying at the retreat. Is that why you're here?'

'I have to admit, it's not, but I'm not sure what I am doing here,' I said.

'Well, why not have a cup of tea with us?' He had a gentle Scottish accent, that was soft and soothing.

'OK, thanks.' He boiled a kettle, put two spoonsful of loose-leaf tea into a large brown teapot with a chipped spout and added the hot water as it came to the boil.

'How long have you been staying here?' I asked Jenna.

She gestured to me to sit down.

I perched on a worn easy chair and she sat on the equally threadbare sofa at the other side of the fireplace.

'Two weeks. It's the most amazing place,' she said.

'It's a retreat?' I asked.

Jenna nodded. 'It is. Anyone can visit when they need time and space away from life.'

'That sounds fantastic. It must be booked up way in advance.'

The man handed me a mug of tea. 'No. People just come.'

'You should stay,' Jenna said. 'Whatever issue has brought you here, it'll be fixed by the time you leave.'

'How do you know I've got an issue?'

'You're here,' Jenna said.

'And all the way from Croydon,' the man said, passing a mug to Jenna.

I was immediately on edge. 'How do you know that?'

'This is a small island. Lorna described a visitor from Croydon when I saw her at the shop. I used to live in London, so she thought I might know you.' He laughed.

'If you are going to stay, I can take your hire car back to Sumburgh on my way through,' Jenna said.

How did she know my car needed to go back to Sumburgh?

'You don't need to look surprised. There's only one place the car could have come from, with the journey you've done,' she said.

'But I don't know how long I'll be here. And what happens when I need to get back?'

'Oh, someone will turn up with a car. They always do,' the man said. 'Or someone will offer you a lift.'

'I arrived three weeks ago from Dulwich,' Jenna said. 'The entire community knowing your business freaked me out when I arrived, but you get used to it surprisingly quickly.'

'What brought you here from Dulwich?'

She licked her lower lip. 'The need to re-evaluate.'

I was torn. I wanted to ask her lots of questions but it seemed a bit cheeky, given I didn't know her. 'And have you re-evaluated?'

'I know exactly what I want to do with my life now, thanks to Farlan.'

'What's Farlan? Some kind of meditation technique?'

The man laughed. 'It's not a what, it's a who. I'm Farlan.' He sat down next to Jenna on the sofa.

I blushed. 'I'm sorry. I didn't realise it was a name.'

'It means "son of the furrows". Not that I've ever ploughed anything in my life.'

'How long have you run this retreat?' I took a sip of my tea.

'A couple of years now. I gave up my London medical practice to come here.'

'You're a doctor?' I asked.

'A psychiatrist,' he said.

'Oh.' I wondered what he made of me.

'Do you want to stay, Lucy?' he asked.

I looked directly at him and he had the deepest brown eyes that were the colour of the darkest chocolate. Their intensity reminded me of the fox's stare.

'I...I don't know.' I felt a bit blindsided.

'Do you want me to show you around?' Jenna asked.

'Sure.' I put my mug onto the arm of the chair and stood up.

'Come this way,' she said. At the end of the main room was a corridor. She pushed open the door into the first room and I stepped inside. Every wall was obscured by shelves of books. The shelves were a dark wood and the books a mixture of old and new-ish. There were two easy chairs at the far end, as old and worn as the furniture in the main room. There were other freestanding bookcases arranged in the middle of the room, all crammed full. It was like going into a library, albeit a ramshackle, higgledy-piggledy one. I picked up the nearest book to me – *Frankenstein* by Mary Shelley – and imagined myself sitting in one of the chairs, devouring it in one sitting.

'I spent a lot of time in here, in between walking and writing,' Jenna said.

'Are you a writer?'

'Not at all. It's part of the learning process, articulating your thoughts.'

'Does Farlan prescribe what you do?'

'He doesn't do anything like that. He leaves you to decide how to spend your time. But he's there to talk to if you need him, as a sounding board, a sympathetic ear. As well as making sure you've got everything you need – food, warmth, whisky.'

'How much does it cost to stay?' I had some money but retreats like this, with a psychiatrist thrown in, must be expensive.

'He doesn't charge.'

'What?'

'I gave him money towards food but the bed and the advice are free.'

'The bed?' I wondered if there was something creepy going on.

'Let me show you.' She walked along the corridor to a door with a 'Guest' name plaque stuck on it – one of those old-fashioned china ones you see in tacky seaside gift shops. It was a small room with a single bed, a chest of drawers and a bedside table. 'This would be your room. The bathroom's next door. Farlan's room is the one at the end.'

It was nice, if basic. 'What's the catch?'

'That's Croydon thinking.'

'Why does he do it if he's not earning money from it?'

'He's a kind man. I'm sure he's got his own demons, his reasons, but I think he's on retreat as much as the rest of us.'

'What's he retreating from?' I was bitten by curiosity.

'He'll tell you if he wants to. He's a bit vulnerable right now, so I'm glad you're here. I think it's good if he's not alone. That's if you're staying?'

'I'll be honest, Jenna. It seems too good to be true.'

'Did the fox bring you here?'

My stomach clenched with discomfort and I hesitated. But for her to know about the fox, well, that must mean she'd had a similar experience. 'Yes.'

'It seems to be able to find souls in need. People for Farlan to help.' She walked back to the main room and I followed.

Farlan looked up. 'Why not go with Jenna to Lorna's place and have a think on the way? You can come here when your booking runs out at the house but only if you want to, Lucy. Maybe if you want to keep your car, you could give Jenna a lift to the ferry terminal.'

'OK,' I was glad to be offered some breathing space. 'Thanks for the tea, Farlan. It was nice to meet you.' I offered my hand.

He shook it and the warmth and strength that flowed from him was both energising and comforting.

Chapter 5

I stepped out of the front door so Jenna could say goodbye to Farlan privately then walked with Jenna back to the house I'd rented. It was a surprisingly short distance but then she knew the direct route.

'Was there someone here when you arrived?' I asked her. 'Someone else using the retreat?'

She nodded. 'A guy called Danny. I recognised him off the TV, some actor from a show, years back, can't remember which one. He'd had a breakdown, he said but Farlan had helped him work out what to do with his life. He took my hire car back to Sumburgh.'

As we neared the house, I asked Jenna why she'd dared to go and stay at a place she knew nothing about with a strange man.

'I felt I'd been led here by something out of the ordinary and I was meant to be here. I took a leap of faith to go with it. And Farlan, well, he seemed so honourable, so decent. I'll be honest, I had a similar conversation with Danny. He'd been visited by the fox and had found his way to the island, like I had. And like you. But I'm sure there are people who come all this way and don't dare to follow through, plenty more who don't even dare to travel. But you've got to ask yourself, Lucy, why would you travel all the way here on the basis of a supernatural event if you're not prepared to go with it?'

'Supernatural?'

'Come on, a disappearing fox that leaves you a key? If that's normal in Croydon, you've been smoking something.' She laughed. 'I did check with Lorna, too, before I decided to stay. The retreat's been running for a while now and people come and go. No-one disappears or has anything nasty happen to them. I think she and the other people who live here wonder a bit about how people know to come, but as far as they're concerned, Farlan's a guy running some kind of religious retreat.'

'It's not religious though, is it?' That wouldn't be my cup of tea at all.

'No, but it is spiritual. It's a special place. You're lucky to be here.'

There is a time in your life for hesitation and a time for action. I didn't want to get this wrong. I'd stay in the house for the remaining two nights and decide when I saw Lorna whether to go to Farlan's retreat.

We arrived at the house. 'Shall I take the car? Or will you give me a lift to the ferry?'

'What time's your ferry?'

'About an hour.'

'Do you want a drink?' I asked.

'You mean, booze? No, thanks. Just in case I'm driving.'

'Tea or coffee, then?'

'Black coffee, thanks.'

I opened up the house and she followed me into the kitchen, leaving her rucksack by the front door. I filled up the kettle and she sat on the sofa while I searched for the coffee.

'Try that cupboard, top right.' She pointed where she meant.

I found it where she'd suggested. 'Did you stay here, too? Before the retreat?'

'Yeah. I stayed here for a week before I found the cottage.'

'What did you do for a week here on your own?'

'I put the shop takings through the roof with my wine bill.' She flushed with embarrassment.

'Don't worry. I'll probably keep them just as well patronised.'

'Not when you're with Farlan.'

'Do you mean he won't let me?' I was sure she'd mentioned whisky earlier.

'He'll let you do whatever you want. But if you're like me, you won't feel the need when you're there.'

I couldn't imagine not wanting a glass of wine or two in the evening. The kettle switched itself off after boiling and the noise startled me. I poured her a coffee and made myself a cup of tea.

'Thanks. It's hard to describe. It's a place where you'll feel as though every need is being met.'

She was selling this a bit too hard. It must have showed in my face.

'Sorry, I must sound a bit OTT. I can see you're suspicious. You'll get out of it what you get out of it. I guess it must be different for everyone. I hope it works for you. That you feel healed by the end.'

'I don't need healing.'

'We all need healing in some way, don't we? And the fact that you're here…' She took a sip of her coffee. 'There must be a reason you came up here. It's a hell of a long way to come from Croydon if you don't feel like something's missing in your life, some gap to be filled, some pain to be soothed.'

'Most likely, some boredom to be eradicated.' Was that it? Was it that my life lacked adventure? 'You said you re-evaluated your life. How?'

She chewed the inside of her lip.

'It's OK. You don't have to tell me.'

'I was in an abusive relationship,' she said, after a pause.

I felt my eyes widen. 'Abusive? Physically or mentally?'

'Both.'

'Are you moving out of your place when you get home? Or kicking someone out?'

She smiled. 'No need.'

I frowned and hoped she'd elucidate.

'I was my own abuser.'

'What? How can you abuse yourself?'

'Self-harm. Alcohol abuse. Constant negativity, beating myself up all the time. Treating myself like I was the worst person in the world.'

'And Farlan cured you?' I heard the crassness of my words and grimaced.

'In a way. Because he made me see that's what I was doing. Not cured, exactly but informed and armed with ways to tackle it. And that's a good start to finding a better way of living.'

I looked at my watch. 'Can you give me a second?' I went into the bathroom and locked the door. Was I going to go and stay at this retreat? Should I take a chance? I checked my jeans pocket for a loose coin. Nothing but an old sweet wrapper. I looked around the bathroom for something I could flip like a coin. Tossing a coin was my "go to" decision-making tool. If the wrong answer came up, I knew my instinct would tell me to flip again. There wasn't anything suitable. But if I needed to toss a coin, that told me enough about my reticence to go to the retreat.

'I should probably think about getting you across to the ferry. I'll give you a lift.'

'Are you sure? Have I freaked you out by being too enthusiastic?'

'I need a bit more time to think.'

She shrugged. 'OK.'

I picked up the car keys and put on my jacket.

As I drove to the ferry, I was overcome by an overwhelming feeling of dread. It was like a black cloud appearing over me and I could feel tension in the back of my head. I pulled up a few yards away from where Jenna would need to get on.

For some reason, my dad came to mind. Outwardly, he had looked like all the other dads at school events but he had an adventurous heart that made him stand out from all the rest. His favourite phrase was "The biggest risk is taking no risk at all". He'd said it to me when I'd had to make a decision about staying at my current school or going to the school for high flyers. And when I couldn't decide whether to drive around Great Britain in a camper van with a friend or fly around the world alone. He'd wanted me to be brave and bold and not be fearful. And I knew he'd want me to go to the retreat, as much as I knew he wouldn't have approved of my safe little life in Croydon. Fuck it. 'Fuck it,' I said out loud.

'You can take the car.' I had to take a chance and go to the retreat, even though I didn't think I needed curing of anything.

We got out of the car and Jenna gave me a hug. 'You won't regret it. Take my number. Ring if you want to talk.'

I punched her number into my phone contacts.

'Remember, to get the best out of this experience, you have to be as honest as you can be. Particularly with yourself.'

I hoped I hadn't lost the ability to tell myself the truth. She drove onto the ferry and shortly afterwards, it left and she was gone. And with her, the car and my only means of escape from here. But that was rubbish. I could easily walk to the ferry if I wanted to leave.

I told myself not to worry about it. I was born to worry, James said. I could magic up a worry in the most perfect of situations. I felt if I worried about the risk of something happening, it wouldn't actually happen, so I tried to anticipate every conceivable thing that could go wrong to make sure it didn't. Surely the worst thing that could happen was that I didn't get much out of the retreat and went back to Croydon with a feeling I'd wasted my time.

I walked along the road and the sun began to come out. As I got into my stride, I tried to breathe deeply and enjoy the truly fresh air of my surroundings. I had an overwhelming urge to smile and I began to feel the tension at the back of my head easing.

Chapter 6

When I got back to the house, I felt the need to switch my brain off for a few hours, so I could process the decision to stay. The few books in the house were factual so I trawled through the DVDs that were kept in an old chest that doubled up as a coffee table and found cinematic treasure in the guise of the original *Star Wars* trilogy. I decided I would watch them back-to-back, with only a comfort break in between. I munched my way through a large packet of Kettle Chips during the first movie and polished off a bottle of wine and a second family-sized bag of crisps during *The Empire Strikes Back*.

As the credits rolled, I weighed up what to do next. It was coming up for 6pm and would be dark by 7pm. Rather than put on *Return of the Jedi*, I would try and be good and go for another walk. It wasn't raining so I took a brisk dash to the southern coastline, which was only a few minutes from the house. I walked along the edge of the land. I came to a site of a natural stone arch, which I remembered was called the Snap, though I had no idea why it was called that. I walked above the arch and the waves glided in and out in all their white-edged beauty. There were dark clouds in the distance and with the wind, it wasn't long before those clouds had reached the island and it started to drizzle. I was about to turn around and dash back to the safety of the cottage when a figure appeared in the distance. It was a man, based on the height and body shape. The wind changed direction suddenly. A noise was being carried in the stiff breeze. It was someone wailing and must have been that lonely figure. The noise was desperate, reminding me of news stories of foreign tragedies, where bereaved people articulated their grief in moans and shouts. It was a sound alien to my English ears. As a nation, we bottle up our loss and weep apologetically in private, too embarrassed to share our raw emotion in public. At least I did.

I half-ran back to the house so I didn't get too wet and once I'd taken my coat off and lit the fire, I took another bottle of white wine out of the fridge and poured myself a glass. I drank it quickly, wanting the effect rather than the taste to dull the headache that still remained from the effects of the first bottle. After one glass, I felt more mellow. The wailing had disturbed me, stirring up memories of my parents' death. They'd been on their retirement holiday, celebrating the end of their working life by travelling around Europe in a newly-acquired camper van they'd nicknamed Tilly. Tilly had ended up going over the edge of a ravine on the French side of the Pyrenees. The police decided it was an accident rather than a deliberate act by persons unknown and it would have been impossible to prove either way. The bodies were flown back to England and it had all felt very distant to me, as though it was happening to someone else. I was damp-eyed at the funeral but held it together. My sister, Sarah, read out what was a very dull eulogy. From her description of them, we'd had different upbringings. Being the first-born, she was the one they tried to protect from everything. They'd tried to stop her doing anything exciting, from the sounds of it. By the time I unexpectedly turned up, they'd gone the opposite way. I was left to find my own path, to make mistakes and to learn from the consequences of my actions in my own time. I almost envied her their stifling kind of love, because I'd often wondered if they loved me at all. They'd looked after me but somehow, I'd felt I was in the way of them having a good time.

A few months after the funeral, I'd been hit by the loss. They were, in fact, ideal parents, letting me live my life, urging me to be as adventurous as they were but being there for me if I needed them while never openly judging my choices. And with that revelation, I had made noises like the wailing man. In private, of course.

I'd met James shortly after that. It had been nice to feel safe and wanted and I'd never dared let go of that security blanket.

I went to bed with a large glass of water, having polished off the second bottle of wine too quickly. I refilled the water glass twice in the night but still woke up with the horrible pressure-filled headache that too much alcohol leaves behind. I'd never learn.

I started to feel vaguely human after I'd showered and dressed. I didn't feel like breakfast so I laid on the sofa and watched *Return of the Jedi*. I went out briefly, walking to Houbie to pick up a sandwich from the café and some more wine and crisps from the shop. I wasn't much in the mood for engaging with the outside world, but I managed to be polite to the shop assistant, who asked my plans. I told her I was going to the retreat in the morning.

'I'm sure you'll have a peaceful time there.' She handed me my card receipt.

I took it as a good sign, that she offered no negative response to the idea of me going to stay with Farlan. But of course, I wanted to believe it would be OK, so even if she had been a bit negative, I'd probably have ignored it.

When I got back, I watched *Toy Story* and *Shrek.* A huge part of me felt guilty at wasting time when I was on a beautiful island where I could be out sightseeing but I craved down time. It was a decompression zone before I went to the retreat where I wasn't sure what I was going to do or find out about myself. I fell asleep on the sofa and had to drag myself to bed around midnight. It was no surprise to me that I felt terrible, given I'd eaten barely anything healthy but I was on holiday, I said to myself in justification.

I woke just after 7am, feeling a bit hungover. I packed my bag as well as all the food and drink I had left over from my trips to the shop. Lorna was due at 10am to pick up the keys so I sat and fidgeted with my phone, checking out Facebook, Twitter and Instagram. It was odd to see my online world of faux friends carrying on without me. People were moaning about late trains or heavy traffic, fawning over pictures of their pets or children, or posting affirmations to try and seem witty or clever. I'd never been good at social media, so I didn't miss it, though I'd wasted plenty of my time looking at it. Ali had posted more pictures of her with her baby. She looked tired but happy. As I switched my focus to Twitter, I felt anew the disappointment that my tweets never got liked by anyone. My phone rang. It was a little after 8am.

'Luce, do you know where my passport is?' James asked, without a hello or a how are you or anything.

'It's in the usual place, with all the other important documents in the filing cabinet in the study.'

'Do you know when it expires?'

'No idea. Why?'

'There's talk of another footie trip and I had a panic it was expiring soon. Thought you might know.'

'I don't, sorry.' Why was I apologising?

'OK. You alright?'

'Yeah, fine.'

'Right. Gotta go. Bye.' He ended the call.

I stared at the phone and shook my head. I suppose I should be grateful he'd asked how I was. My mind drifted to the first time we'd met and how nice he'd seemed. How keen he was to spend time with me. He'd never been demonstrative of his feelings but I had to wonder how he felt about me now.

A knock on the door surprised me. It was only 8:30am. Surely Lorna wouldn't be that early. I got up and opened the door.

'Morning.' It was Farlan.

'Bloody hell. What are you doing here?' I could hear my voice was in full Croydon mode - suspicious and wary.

He raised his eyebrows. 'A foolish thing, clearly. Offering my car so you don't have to walk your luggage up to the cottage or to the ferry terminal, whichever you've decided is your destination.'

I flushed with embarrassment. 'That's kind of you. Sorry if I sounded rude.' I remembered Jenna telling me to be as truthful as possible. 'I sounded rude because I was being rude. I couldn't help but be suspicious that you have ulterior motives.'

He gave a deep-throated laugh. 'That's a refreshingly honest answer.'

'Do you have an ulterior motive?'

'My motivation stems from wanting to help anyone who finds their way here.'

'But why? Why should you care about me or anyone else that turns up on your doorstep?'

'It's human nature to care about others.' He gave me the full Farlan stare.

I held his gaze. 'People you know, yes. But not complete strangers.'

'Sometimes, it's easier to help a stranger than someone you're close to.'

I sort of understood that. There'd be too much baggage with friends and family.

'Have you decided where you want to go? Cottage or Croydon? Or somewhere else entirely, of course.'

'Sorry, why don't you come in?' I was suddenly aware he was on the doorstep and it was cold out.

'OK.' He looked bemused.

'Can I make you a cup of tea or something?'

He shook his head. 'I had one before I came across. Is there anything you'd like to ask me?'

'I suppose there is,' I invited him to sit down on the blue sofa. I took the easy chair next to it so I could look at him properly. He was tall, maybe 6'2'' and muscular, broad at the shoulders but lean in the hips. He had thick dark hair that was starting to grey at the temples. I guessed he was in his late thirties, about the same age as James. The parts of his face that weren't hidden by his beard looked worn in places, like a piece of material that's gone shiny through use. And of course, there were those eyes. Dark, yet curiously welcoming. If I was honest, he was attractive in a brooding, taciturn, action hero kind of way. How Braveheart should have looked in the movie, probably.

'Fire away,' he said.

I smiled and tried to work out what I wanted to say, to ask him. I chewed my lip for inspiration.

'Do you have questions about the retreat? Or the people who visit? Or me?'

'I suppose I don't feel broken, so I'm not sure what needs fixing.'

'You're not a toaster, Lucy. Change the element and you'll be back in working order. Humans aren't built like that.'

'I guess I don't feel like there's anything wrong, anything about my life that I need to change, so would I be wasting your time or taking up space in the retreat when there's someone out there who needs your help?'

'Don't you think you're important enough to stay there?' He looked at me, eyes flitting up and down.

'It's not about importance. At least I don't think it is, but if I was a toaster, I wouldn't want to take it to the repair shop and for them to say it's in working order. That would be wasting their time.' I wasn't making much sense.

'Lucy, the fact you're here is a sign you want something different. Perhaps you need some time away from home to work out why you want something different. Maybe even work out what it is you do want.'

I could feel my dad pushing me out of here. 'That sounds OK, yeah.' I gestured with my hand towards the door. 'Lead on, MacDuff.'

He looked at me and smiled. 'Bit of a Shakespeare fan?'

'Enough of one to know I'm misquoting Shakespeare, but it's an apposite phrase.'

He stood up and pointed to the shopping bags. 'Shall I put these in the car?'

'Yes, please.'

He lifted them as though they weighed nothing. The wine bottles clanked together and I blushed.

'You and Jenna would have got on.' He gave me a mischievous grin.

I followed him, opening the front door so he could put the bags in his car, a battered Volvo Estate that had more scratches on it than a child with chickenpox. I put my suitcase onto the back seat.

'You can leave the keys in the house,' he said.

'Shouldn't I lock it?'

'Lorna will be here soon enough and who's around to go in?'

He was right. I needed to stop thinking like a Londoner and more like an islander.

Chapter 7

Farlan drove us to a spot that was apparently not too far from the cottage. 'It's too wet underfoot to go any nearer.' He got out of the car and picked up both shopping bags in one hand and my suitcase in the other.

I followed him up to the cottage door, carrying only my handbag. 'Thanks. That's kind of you.'

We went inside and he put my bags down by the front door. He threw something on the fire and it sprung into flame.

I found a real fire mesmerising and went towards it.

'Why don't you get yourself settled into the guest room while I move the car? Should be back in about fifteen minutes.' He strode out of the front door and peace descended.

I was pleased to have some time to explore the place alone. I went toward the small kitchen area so I could put the milk in the fridge, but I couldn't find anything resembling a fridge. I spotted a carton of milk and a pot of cream on the floor by what must have been a back door at some point and when I put my hand on the carton, it felt chilled, so I put the milk and cheese next to the cream and lined up my bottles of white wine there too. I left the rest of the shopping in its bag and put it by a small cupboard next to the wall.

I went to the guest room with my suitcase. The bedding was freshly laundered and I wondered where Farlan had been able to do that. If he hadn't got a fridge, there certainly wasn't going to be a washing machine tucked away. But in such a damp environment, how could he dry the bedding?

I went back into the main room. I'd sat on the dog-eared armchair on my first visit so I tried the sofa. My phone managed to get one bar of signal in the bedroom but it was better in the main room, particularly if I stood by one of the windows. It was good to know I could make a phone call if needed.

Farlan appeared a few minutes later. He hung up his coat on a hook near the fire and gave me a glass with a finger of amber liquid in it. I assumed it was whisky and took a sip. I wasn't keen on the taste but the warmth from it and the fire made me feel relaxed and my mind drifted to the point when the fox's eyes had first gazed on me.

'Have a think about how you want to spend your time today.' Farlan's voice interrupted my daydream. There was something calming about its tone. 'You like to read. And write too, I think. You'll have plenty of opportunity to do both here. And to walk, to give you time to think about the future.'

'It sounds idyllic.' I took another sip of whisky. I felt at peace, as though someone had lifted my worries off my shoulders a little while I was sitting there. I'd not been particularly observant when I'd first arrived, so I looked around. The room was homely, with sheepskin rugs on the floor and wall-hangings of thick brightly-coloured thread, woven into intricate patterns. It was quite light, now the curtains had been pulled back, and had windows on three sides.

Farlan was watching me. 'Do you want some more?'

I shook my head. 'It's a bit early in the day, even for me.'

'Tea, then?'

SON OF THE FURROWS

I nodded and he went to the kitchen area. I sat and waited, wondering what would happen next.

He handed me a mug with the bottom half of the handle missing.

'Thank you.' The tea was strong, the colour of one of those old-fashioned toffees that take out your fillings, but it tasted lovely. 'How long have you lived here?'

'Feels like forever but I kind of came on retreat like you, from elsewhere, and couldn't leave.' He rubbed his chin as if he was thinking.

'Couldn't leave? Do you mean you couldn't? Or you didn't want to?'

'Didn't want to. But don't forget, Lucy, you can leave anytime you want. The door is always open. I can make sure you get back to Houbie or the ferry. But I don't think that's what you want.'

'How do you know?'

'Well, it seems clear you don't want your life in Croydon.'

'I might. Maybe I need a break from it.' As I said it, I sensed that wasn't true. And by the look on his face, Farlan didn't think that either.

'I've got a bit of work to do this morning so I'll leave you here, if that's OK?' he asked.

'Sure.'

'Why not spend some time in the library? Take your tea with you.'

'I will. See you later, then.' I got up and walked to the far end of the library after retrieving the Frankenstein volume I'd seen the day before. There was a blanket on the arm of each chair and I wrapped myself in one, draped myself over the chair and opened the book. I felt like a child again, free to read for as long as I wanted.

Farlan peered around the door. 'Do you need anything else, Lucy?'

'I don't think so. Thank you.'

'I shall leave you to Mary.' He closed the door behind him.

I buried myself in the book, living every moment, inhabiting every scene in a way you can only do when you've enough time available to devote yourself entirely to a book. As I came to the end, I needed the loo and was feeling hungry.

I took off the woollen blanket and went down the corridor. I found the bathroom and wasn't in the least bit surprised when the toilet flush made more creaking noises than a haunted house on *Scooby Doo*. I couldn't resist carrying on the tour of the house, as there was only one door left that I hadn't seen properly. Jenna had said it was Farlan's room. It was slightly ajar and I peeked through the inch-gap. Farlan was sitting on the bed with his back to me, naked from the waist up. There were long, deep scars across his back. I couldn't help myself and I gasped at the sight.

He was up and at the door in a second. He stared at me without saying anything.

I felt compelled to speak. 'Sorry. I didn't realise you were here. I didn't mean to pry.'

He looked down then back up at me. 'I want you to feel at home here, so you shouldn't feel like you're prying. It works best for us both if there are no secrets. I've come back for some lunch. You must have been engrossed in your book and not heard me.' He smiled.

There was something enigmatic about him. Mysterious and a bit scary. No, not scary. Fierce. He was glorious with all those scars, like someone from another world, another time. And he had a library. In a small cottage, a library was his priority. How brilliant was that?

'How do you make money? How do you live?' I asked.

'I have income from a property I inherited. It's enough to live on.'

'Even with your insatiable book habit?'

He gave a smile and nodded. 'Even with that.' He picked up a shirt that was hooked on the back of the bedroom door and put it on. 'Would you like to go for a walk?'

'Can I get something to eat first?'

'Of course. I hope you like porridge.'

'I...well, I've only ever had it in a "ready to microwave" pot.'

'Then you've never really had porridge.' He gestured with his head and we walked back into the main room and into the kitchen area. He heated up some porridge on a small ring.

'Don't you have an oven?'

He shook his head. 'Never bothered. I can cook fine on this.' He put a large dollop of hot porridge into a bowl and added a drizzle of cream and a dash of whisky. There was a small drop-leaf table by the wall, which he opened on one side. He pulled a folding wooden chair from behind the solitary kitchen cupboard and made a gesture for me to sit down. He placed the bowl of still-steaming porridge in front of me. 'I hope you like it.' He began eating straight from what was left in the pot.

I tried a little, guessing it was going to be luscious with the cream and whisky. 'Gosh, that's gorgeous. Thank you.' I devoured spoon after spoon of it and felt ready for anything by the time I'd scraped the bowl clean.

He put the dirty dishes in the sink. 'I'll sort those later.'

'Where do you wash your clothes?'

'Lorna lets me use the facilities in the big house, next to the one you were staying in. Small stuff I can dry by the fire but it's a struggle with sheets.'

'That's kind of her.'

'Community thrives on kindness. You can't be in a place like this and be isolated from the rest of the people here. You have to help each other.'

I liked that philosophy, though I still hadn't got my head around people knowing your every move. Maybe I'd get used it, like Jenna had said.

Chapter 8

Farlan and I walked for a couple of hours. I began to get a sense of the terrain. We didn't see anyone on our walk, though we did spot some seals playing at the water's edge.

Apart from pointing out some key landmarks, including a low stone circle and various flora and fauna, Farlan didn't speak. He obviously didn't do small talk, which suited me, as I was rubbish at it, but you didn't need it here. It was such a lovely place to be. When the sun shone, it was like being bathed in gold.

'We should get back,' he said. 'Storm's coming in.'

It looked glorious to my untrained eye but it did darken as we neared the cottage and within a few minutes of getting back, I could hear rain tapping on the windows.

'What would you like to do before dinner?' he asked. 'How about some writing?'

'How do you know I write?' I tried to make sure my voice sounded free of suspicion.

'Instinct. Let me show you the writing room.'

I thought I'd seen all the rooms in the place but there was a door I'd missed around the corner from the main corridor. It was like a large cupboard, but it had a window with a small desk in front of it and a chair like the one I'd sat on in the kitchen. There were notebooks and paper on a shelf underneath the desk. A wooden pot full of pens and pencils was on the windowsill.

'It's basic but if you want to write, you can do it here.'

'Thank you.' There was something oddly atmospheric about the room, but I wasn't sure why. Perhaps it was the absence of technology. As Farlan closed the door, it felt as though I could climb inside my mind here, search out all the ideas I'd had over the years for stories and novels and put them on paper. I picked up a pen, opened the first notebook in the pile and felt an overwhelming urge to put fiction aside and write about Croydon, to document everything about it that made me unhappy.

The first thing that came to mind was James's verbal cruelty towards me, his taunting and snide comments. It was at its worst when we were in our local pub, where he liked to hang out with his mates and watch the footie on a Saturday. I used to dread him inviting me along. If his team won, it was OK. He would enjoy several pints with his friends and they'd dissect the game with the precision of a vet removing a chihuahua's gonads. I was largely forgotten and would happily daydream till it was time to go home. But if his team lost, and they did, quite often, his anger and frustration at the result seemed to come back on me. At first, I tried to be whatever it was he wanted me to be at that point, be it one of the lads, joining in with the frustrated rants or his partner in crime, offering sympathy and buying the drinks. If I joined in with the puerile banter, it rarely had a positive effect. James would tell me I was being stupid, or that my jokes were pathetic. He once told me to fuck off. Even this far away from home, I could feel myself colouring at the thought of it, as I wrote down what used to happen. His friends used to give me this pitying look, every time James started on me. But they'd never say anything to challenge his behaviour. It was as though they thought it was my fault, too. I suppose I was a convenient whipping boy for all of them. I'd stopped going to the pub with him after he told me to piss off home once too often. He pleaded with me to go with him after that, said he liked having me there, but he'd never apologised for his words or for how he'd treated me. He tried to make out I was over-reacting or that I couldn't take a joke. In the safety of Farlan's writing room, I tried to document how it had made me feel. I wrote as quickly as I could. I didn't want to dwell on it. I would read it later.

After a couple of hours, I paused, my hand aching as it used to in school exams. As I sat back, I couldn't recall what I'd written, so I turned to the first page of the notebook and began to read.

'Lucy, are you OK?' Farlan's voice broke through into the room, shattering the solitary atmosphere.

I blinked back tears. I could barely see from crying.

'Can I come in?' he asked.

'Yeah,' was all I could manage.

The door opened and he looked at me with his fox's eyes. Seeing my distress, he bent down and gave me an enormous, enveloping hug. It was one of the loveliest hugs I'd ever had. I felt like a baby being cradled by its father. I had a feeling of absolute safety.

'Do you feel better for that?' He gestured towards the notebook.

I gulped to try and swallow the stirred emotions. 'Kind of. It's hit me. How unhappy I was though I never felt unhappy. Bored, maybe. Unfulfilled, definitely. But not unhappy. Now I realise I've been craving something I wasn't getting from my life.'

'That's what brought you here.' He stepped back. 'I'm going to make up the fire now. It's chilly out and the cottage will get cold if I don't. Shall we have dinner followed by an evening of telling each other ghost stories by firelight?'

My face broke into a smile and I could feel the residue of tears on my lips. I rubbed them away and could taste their salt. 'That sounds wonderful.' I let out a hiccup.

He laughed and left the room. It was a lovely sound, his laugh. It was low and came from deep within him. I went to the bathroom to tidy up my face after my crying fest and was surprised to see how much happier the person staring back at me looked. How could I have not noticed how miserable I'd been?

By the time I went back to the main room, the fire was throwing out heat and I could smell something cooking. Farlan looked up at me. 'I've some stew. We can sit by the fire and eat if you like.'

I nodded and sat down on the hearth rug while he finished the preparations for dinner. It was quite early but it was getting dark outside, or at least the lowering clouds were making it seem so. There was no sound in the cottage, save the occasional scraping of metal on metal as Farlan stirred the stew and a more frequent whistling of the wind under the front door. I noticed I didn't have the terrible knot in my stomach that I'd had for the last few months, particularly before food. It was from getting stressed about James judging me for what or how much I was about to eat. He would often mansplain about diet and exercise, shaking his head at me for every excess calorie, not seeing the hypocrisy of his position, given he'd sink several G&Ts and a bottle of wine in an evening without a thought. When he'd had a drink, his comments to me would get more unpleasant with each sip.

'I thought you were feeling better,' Farlan said as I took the proffered bowl of stew.

'Why do you ask?'

'Your face.'

'I do feel better. I was thinking about something in the past.'

'It would be a good idea to try and put it behind you.' He crossed his legs and sat down in a single, athletic movement.

I envied him the flexibility and strength to be able to do that. I'd have ended up in an untidy heap on the rug if I'd tried it.

'Have I got something on my nose?' He rubbed his face.

I must have been staring too long. 'No. I'm jealous of your abilities.'

'Which ones? You've not tasted the stew yet so it can't be my cooking.'

I ate a spoonful of meat and gravy. It was delicious, deeply flavoured and satisfying.

'Oh, that's lush. Now I'm envious of your cooking skills too.'

'Don't be. I got the stew off one of the islanders. Swapped it for a book.' He grinned.

'You cheat.' I laughed. 'I hope you're not going to give away too many books before I've had a chance to read them.'

'I wouldn't worry. I can't resist getting more. There'll always be a full library here.'

I felt emboldened by the stew and the firelight. 'What do you do to keep yourself fit? I know you said you have money from a property but you can't sit in here eating porridge all day, not with a body like yours.' I felt myself blushing and he was quick to pick up on it.

'You a bit too close to the fire there? Those cheeks of yours look burnished.' He raised his eyebrows in a way that told me he was ribbing me.

'Don't deflect.'

'I help with building and renovation projects, mainly. It gives me some cash in hand and as you say, keeps me fit.'

'You must be hoping Brough Lodge gets sold. That'll be one hell of a building project.'

He nodded. 'Enough?' He gestured towards my now-empty bowl.

'Thank you, yes.'

He took the bowl and got up from his cross-legged position by pushing his body upwards. 'What?'

'Nothing. I envy you being able to do that.'

'You can do it. Cross your legs now.'

I shook my head.

He put the bowls on the easy chair and went behind where I was sitting, squatting directly behind me. 'Come on.'

I crossed my legs and he put his arms under my armpits. 'Right, on three. One, two, three.'

I pushed with my feet and he lifted me up as I did so. 'I don't think that counts.'

'But you get the idea of what you need to do. If you practise, you'll be able to do it unaided. As with most things in life, it depends how badly you want it, Lucy.' He was still holding me under the arms and he was speaking by my right ear, close enough for me to feel his breath on my neck and ear. It made me shiver, in a nice way, but that seemed to spook him. He moved his arms and, in a moment, had picked up the bowls and was washing them in the sink.

'Can I help with anything?'

'No, you're fine. Stay in front of the fire, or go and get a book if you want.' He seemed to be scrubbing the bowls hard enough to take the pattern off.

'You promised me ghostly tales.'

'Hmm, OK,' He washed the pot he'd heated the stew in and finished tidying the kitchen.

Chapter 9

Farlan brought a bottle of whisky and two glasses over to the fire, poured a small amount in each glass and handed one over to me. He sat at the opposite end of the hearth rug, with his back against the sofa. 'Slàinte Mhath, as we say around here.' He raised his glass.

'Same to you.' I didn't want to try and repeat the unfamiliar words and waved my glass in the air. Instead of warming me, the whisky tasted sour. I wondered if the sourness was actually within me. I put the glass down beside me and picked at the rug tufts. 'Can I ask you a question?'

He shrugged as if to agree.

'What's with the fox? Are you the fox? Is the fox you?' There. I'd asked.

He chewed the inside of his cheek then looked up at me. 'I'm not sure what I can tell you. And please don't throw back at me what I said about secrets.'

'I'm not the one that said it in the first place.'

'Some things are hard to explain.'

'OK then. Tell me about something Jenna said.'

He looked confused. 'What?'

'She was happy to leave when I arrived because she said she didn't want you to be here alone. Why did she say that?'

'It can be lonely here. Its solitude and isolation, part of what makes it good, is also what makes it not so good if you're in a negative frame of mind.' He was looking at me but not making eye contact. 'We all have demons, Lucy.'

I felt a wave of, what was it? Pity? Sadness? Guilt? A bit of all of them and maybe a deeply buried mothering instinct too. 'If you want to tell me about your demons, then do. I'll listen. But if you don't, that's OK.' I gave him a half-smile, trying to empathise without knowing or understanding his situation.

'I moved from Scotland to go to university in Oxford, did my medical training in London before I started practising. I got bitten by an urban fox when I was living in St John's Wood. Something happened. It died but I seemed to have been possessed by it. The night after, I was in bed, but I found myself out on the streets, as the fox, foraging. At first, I thought it was a dream but it wasn't. It was some kind of out of body experience. It was hard to deal with for a man of science. Still is. I thought if I came up here, got away from everything, it would stop, but it didn't. The fox stayed urban, moving around suburbs, searching out people in need. And I realised that here was the perfect place for people to come and sort out their issues. And so, the retreat came to life. It started out with people from North London then came south. Danny was from Peckham. Jenna was from Dulwich. Then it moved on to Croydon.'

None of this made sense, but I could tell Farlan absolutely believed it. And hell, I knew his eyes matched those of the fox that had been in my garden in Croydon. I'd seen the fox when I first got to the island and I knew that foxes didn't live here. Maybe we were both mad.

'Do you have control over where the fox goes and where it leaves the key?'

'Not control but I think my mind influences the fox in its choices.'

'Let's try and be logical about this. The fox should stop roving when it finds what it wants. Which must mean when you find what you want. What is that, Farlan? What do you want?'

'I don't know, Lucy. Honestly. I don't know.'

'But you want to stay here, don't you? You like it here, at least that's the impression you give.'

'I do. I like the simple life, one with few people and little responsibility. And I like having people come here, to the retreat. I like that I'm given the chance to help them. But I wonder if I'm running away.'

'From what?'

'Like I said, we all have demons.' He reached over to the whisky bottle and half-filled his glass. 'Cheers.' He downed the lot in one. He tried hard not to cough but his eyes watered at the potency of the drink. 'Sorry. That's no answer, is it?'

'No. Please don't do a James.'

'You mean treat you like shit after a few drinks?'

I nodded. 'How do you know?' I bit my bottom lip, feeling exposed.

'Lucky guess. Or rather, it's based on the majority of urban relationships I used to see in London, when I was working there as a psychiatrist.'

'Is that the sort of people you treated?'

'Absolutely not. Most relationships don't need psychiatry. I specialised in working with serial sexual offenders in prison. The relationships I'm talking about were observations of friends and colleagues.'

'I see.' I wondered what his psychiatry training told him about me.

'You've got that look on your face.'

'What look?'

'The one most people have when they hear what I do for a living. They think I'm analysing them and finding them wanting.'

'And are you?'

'Probably.' He laughed.

'Well, I'm sure you'll find me deficient in many ways. That's scarier than any ghost story, the thought of you analysing my sad little life.' I waved my empty glass at him. 'Is there any of that left or have you had it all?'

He passed the bottle over. There was barely enough to cover the bottom of the glass.

'Sorry,' he said.

'Don't be. Not sure I want to get pissed in front of a psychiatrist. Who knows what secrets I'd give away?'

'I don't practise anymore.'

'You still know it all though. Were you struck off?'

'God, no. I just stopped doing it when I came here.'

'How come you haven't analysed yourself? How can you not know what it is you want when you know the right questions to ask?' I sat back. 'Maybe because you do know what you want. And either that's what you've run away from, for some reason. Or…' I puzzled over an alternative. 'Or you don't think you deserve it. So, you hide away up here to make sure you can't get it.'

'Thank you, Doctor Lucy, for that insight.' He gave me a sideways glance. 'And what does the doctor suggest as treatment for my condition?'

'Hmmm, let me think.' I tipped the tiny bit of whisky from my glass into my mouth and chewed all the flavour out of it before swallowing. 'I think you need to analyse the fox, not you. Whatever you've suppressed, whatever it is you're denying yourself, that fox is still trying to find for you. It's an incarnation of your subconscious, I reckon. Work out what he's looking for and you'll know the answer.' I sat back against the chair, feeling pleased that what I'd said sounded plausible at least. He was clearly an intelligent man, to have studied medicine and specialised in psychiatry. I knew I couldn't match him intellectually but I hoped I didn't sound like a fool.

Farlan went quiet. He was staring into the fire, which was glowing with the remnants of whatever it was he was burning. The room was getting colder and it felt as though it wasn't just the temperature. It was as though he was a living, breathing part of this cottage and his drop in emotional temperature affected his home too. I wondered if it was because he was such an imposing individual. He filled the room with his presence, his charisma. Now he'd gone quiet, everything else seemed muted. I'd been hoping to ask him some more questions but it felt as though the time for talking had passed.

SON OF THE FURROWS

I went to sit next to him, put my arm around his shoulder and said nothing. He was staring into space and I wondered if he'd become the fox, wandering somewhere in South London while his human form sat empty. We sat, quite still, silence filling the void like a creeping fog. The fire began to lose its glow and we were soon in near darkness. I tried to pinpoint the feeling I was experiencing, sitting in the dark with my arm around Farlan who was as still as a millpond outwardly but probably churning like a whirlpool inside. Or maybe he wasn't. There was tranquillity in that moment for me, a moment that turned into minutes and felt like hours.

Farlan let out a long breath and came back into the room. 'Thank you.'

I smiled and felt bad at having to stifle a yawn.

'We should get some sleep.' He got up and lit two candles, handing one to me.

I got up, feeling light-headed from the silent interlude. 'Thanks. Will you start analysing me tomorrow?'

'That's not the way it works. If you want to talk or ask questions, you can do that. But if you don't, don't.'

We walked into the corridor and he stopped outside my room. 'I hope it's not too cold for you in there.'

'It'll be fine. Goodnight, Farlan.' I went up on tiptoe and gave him a peck on the cheek.

I closed the door to my room. It felt chilly after being in front of the fire, so I got into bed without bothering to undress. I blew out the candle and wondered how long it would take me to fall asleep.

Chapter 10

I was woken by a tap on my bedroom door. 'There's porridge keeping warm on the stove. I've got to go out for a while.' Farlan's footsteps gradually got quieter and the front door closed with a bang.

I got up and ran a bath. I'd much rather have showered but the cottage didn't stretch to that. I was glad there was some hot water but I didn't know how much and only filled the bath a few inches. I washed myself and my hair as best I could. I thought back to the facilities at the house where I'd been staying. It had Wi-Fi, a good shower and a hairdryer. And a proper kitchen. I wondered if I'd done the right thing, moving to this place that was stuck in the past. I briefly thought about the home comforts of Croydon and wondered if I'd have been better off staying there. But I knew that wasn't true. I'd documented my feelings about my relationship with James the day before and that was enough of a wake-up call for me that change was needed in my life.

I had no idea when Farlan would be back so I decided I could either go for a walk or stay in and read. I went into the library but it was freezing. Sod it. I pulled on my coat and walking boots, borrowed a soft woollen hat from the peg behind the door and left. Five minutes out, I remembered Farlan had said the porridge was keeping warm. I ran back and went inside to turn off the ring. It seemed a waste to leave the porridge, but I didn't feel hungry. It was odd for me, feeling as though I was in touch with my body's needs for the first time in, well, probably ever. I normally ate out of habit, regardless of whether I was hungry or not. If it was a mealtime, I had to eat. But I could hear my body this morning and all it was craving was fresh air. I guessed it was because on Fetlar I had no distractions and was able to tune into my body's wavelength. Normal life made too much noise for me to hear my body's music. But here, I could hear.

I remembered there was no whisky left after Farlan had finished it all last night, so I decided I'd first go to the shop and get him some more.

I left the house again, locking the door with the very key that had led me to the island and set off in the direction I now knew was towards Houbie. I came across a deserted primary school and carried on to the shop. I hadn't thought what time it was. The shop wasn't open. I was a couple of hours early. I decided to walk over to Brough Lodge. It was quiet along the road and the light mist had turned to drizzle. I pulled the hat down over my ears and strode on, taking in deep breathes of the clean, salt-tanged air.

By the time the shop was open, I'd walked to Brough Lodge, back past Houbie and on to Funzie then back to Houbie. The rain had continued to fall, and by the time I went into the shop, I felt cold and a bit miserable from the dampness I felt seeping into my bones.

I wandered slowly around the shop's aisles, enjoying the warmth as I thawed out, chatting with other customers as I browsed. I picked up a few sweet treats for myself. They weren't good for me but I knew they would make me feel better for the few seconds I was eating them. And I was on holiday and deserved a treat. I picked up a bottle of whisky for Farlan and a bottle of brandy for me. As I paid, the woman serving asked me where I was staying now.

'With Farlan, at his retreat,' I said. She packed a sturdy jute bag with my bottles. 'This is a great shop.'

'Thanks. There aways seems to be someone on retreat there and they mostly go home happy.'

'Mostly?'

'There's been the odd woman who seemed disappointed she couldn't stay longer.' She raised her eyebrows and smiled.

'I'll have to ask Farlan about that.'

'You have a good day now.' She handed me the bag and I smiled at her.

I regretted having bought two bottles without bringing a rucksack to carry them in. Walking across the uneven land with a bag in one hand made progress slow. As I got to within sight of the cottage, I could see Farlan outside. He seemed to be waiting.

'You took the key,' he said.

'I took my key. You've got yours.'

He shook his head.

I knew I'd seen two keys the day before. 'Have you already given your key to someone else? Have you been out on one of your foxy jaunts and found someone more interesting to move in? Will they be turning up soon in a hire car that I have to take back to Sumburgh?' I turned my back on him and opened the door.

'Lucy! Why are you angry?'

'I'm not.' Despite being someone who wasn't looking for a retreat and wasn't fussed about staying and didn't feel broken, I felt cheated by the idea that someone was already being lined up to take my place. I took the bottle of whisky out of the bag and put it on the side table by the door, before telling Farlan I was going into the library. The rest of my shopping came with me and I closed the library door with a bang.

I pulled the easy chairs together so I could sit on one and put my feet on the other, and settled down with two Jane Austen novels that I knew off by heart. I drank brandy and ate two bars of chocolate while I skim read *Persuasion* then drunk more brandy and ate another chocolate bar as I started to read *Emma*. I was annoyed that Farlan walked past the window at the wrong moment, catching sight of me swigging from the brandy bottle like a wino. Bollocks. I wrapped the blanket more tightly around me and carried on reading.

He came into the library a few minutes later. 'Are you OK, Lucy? Would you like some tea?'

I shook my head, not feeling like talking to him and not wanting to catch his eye. I was scared of saying something stupid, which was what usually happened when I'd had a few drinks.

'I'll leave you to it then. Do you need food or anything?'

'No, thanks.' I kept my eyes firmly on my book, not wanting him to know how much I'd drunk.

He walked out and closed the door.

It was hard to settle. I couldn't work out the mess of feelings in my head. I was afraid I'd be leaving soon, yet I didn't like it here. It was too austere. I didn't believe Farlan liked to live like this. He was surely punishing himself in some way or another. But for what? Whatever his issues, I still needed to work out what I wanted to do with myself. I couldn't hide away up here for ever. Just because I'd worked out Croydon was wrong, didn't make Fetlar right.

When I was half-way through *Emma*, I needed the bathroom and could put it off no longer. I hoped Farlan wasn't around but when I opened the door, he was walking from his room towards the main one, so I couldn't avoid him. I knew it was hurting me to be annoyed with him, so I tried to smile, though I didn't feel much like it with only brandy and chocolate inside me.

He smiled back. 'I didn't get the chance to explain. The second key was in the house. I didn't take it with me when I went out because I thought you'd be here when I got back.'

Of course. I was an idiot and admitted as much to him.

He shrugged. 'It's fine. You're dealing with a lot at the moment.'

'Whatever I'm dealing with is no excuse for being unpleasant to you. I'm sorry.'

'Apology accepted. As a doctor, I'm not sure I recommend this new diet of yours.' He winked.

'I said I was an idiot. I've never broken the habit of thinking that food and alcohol can change the way I feel. And I was feeling positive this morning. I don't know what went wrong.' I cocked my head to one side as rain began to batter the windows. 'I was going to go for a walk to clear my head, but I don't think I fancy going out in that.'

'Yer Southern softie.'

'Yep, and proud. But you're from south of here, too.'

'I was born in the Highlands.'

'Have you got family somewhere around there?'

For a moment, he grimaced with what looked like anguish. 'No close family, not anymore.'

'Have I put my foot in it?'

'You weren't to know. My father died ten days ago.'

'Why didn't you say? I'm terribly sorry.' I gave him a hug without thinking and the penny dropped. 'Is that why Jenna didn't want you to be on your own? Because you're grieving?'

He pulled away but not in a way that felt hostile to my spontaneous gesture. 'It is.'

'So, why are you still here? Why haven't you gone to be with your mother or siblings?'

'Mother's long gone. My little brother died aged four. There is only me.'

'Don't you need to be there? Have you stayed here because of me?'

'No. I do need to go to the funeral in a couple of days, get over there and sort some things out, but the family solicitor is doing most of it.'

'Please don't take this the wrong way. I know I was stupid for getting it wrong about the key and stuff. And I realise that I know the answer to this question already because, well, why would you, but I'll ask anyway. Do you want me to go with you to the funeral? As a friend?'

'Oh, Lucy, that's kind of you.' He went silent for a full minute. 'I don't know how I feel about anything right now.'

Of course, he didn't want me there. 'Well, listen, whenever you go, if you want me to go with you, just ask and I will. If not, I'll wait here, getting drunk on brandy and eating chocolate, till you get back.'

'Is that emotional blackmail?' He said it light-heartedly but went silent again. 'I suppose it would be better to have someone with me than face the demons alone. Yes, please. I'd like you to come with me, if you're sure.'

I nodded. '100% sure.'

'Then I'll book you a flight.'

Chapter 11

I woke up early the next morning and parted the curtains so I could peer out to see what the weather was like. Farlan was outside, dressed in shorts and a sports vest, doing what looked like some form of yoga. I stared unashamedly at his physique. He was muscular but not bulky. His movements were slow and controlled. He held poses that showed his strength and flexibility. Was there anything this man wasn't good at? He must have sensed he was being watched. He stood up from a deep squat that made my thighs ache just to look at it and we made eye contact. He smiled and held up his splayed hand, which I assumed meant he'd be five minutes.

I went to the kitchen and turned on the kettle just as he came in. 'Morning. Tea?'

'No, thanks. I'm going to get a bath. Can you be ready to leave in an hour?'

'Sure. Can you leave the bath water for me when you're finished?'

'Are you sure? You can have fresh water.'

'I don't like hot water so let's be green and share.'

'Share?' He raised an eyebrow.

I felt myself blushing. 'The water, I meant, not the bath.' I looked at his face. 'You're teasing me, aren't you? James said I was the most gullible person he'd ever met.'

'Your default position is to trust everyone. A nice person would see that as a positive. I'll leave the water when I've finished but feel free to run fresh if you want.'

An hour later, we walked to Farlan's car, which was parked near the ferry terminal. He was silent for the journey from island to island. I left him to his own thoughts and tried to marshal mine into some form of order. I knew James wasn't my future but was struggling to work out what was. Croydon, with or without James, wasn't what I wanted anymore. It was too urban, too busy. I wanted somewhere I could hear myself think. If only our working from home policy let you work anywhere.

It took a few hours to get back to Sumburgh and Farlan had booked flights to Inverness from there for us both. I had nothing suitable to wear to a funeral but Farlan had said it was fine as there'd be some clothes at the house I could use. I hoped I wouldn't have to wear an old dress of his mother's but decided to keep quiet and gauge the situation when we arrived.

From Inverness, we went by hire car for nearly an hour and a half. He turned off the road and went down a long driveway to what the sign said was an estate with a name I couldn't pronounce. Perhaps his father had lived in a cottage on the land or something. We pulled up at a fine house that looked like something owned by royalty. A man came out to greet us.

'Mr Alexander. Good to have you back, Sir.'

'McDonald, good to see you. This is Miss Lucy, a friend of mine. Can you put her in one of the guest suites and have Mrs Mac find her something suitable to wear for tomorrow?'

'Of course, sir. Miss, if you'd like to come this way?'

I got out of the car and followed McDonald into the house. Oh my, it was beautiful. It reminded me of when I'd dragged James around the place where they filmed *Downton Abbey*. He'd been utterly bored but I'd thought it was lovely. I was taken up a sweeping wooden staircase that divided in two to feed both left and right parts of the upstairs of this wing of the house. The banister was carved with leaves, acorns, stags' heads and berries and looked stunning. McDonald showed me into a room that had a small four-poster bed with a richly-decorated tapestry draped over the foot end. There was a bathroom next door, he told me, then left me alone. I sat down on a low chair that looked out over the front lawn, unsure what to do next.

Farlan came in a few minutes later with my bag.

'Jeez, Farlan. What is this place?'

'It's my family home.' He said it as though it was the most natural thing in the world. Which I suppose, to him, it was.

'Is Alexander your family name, your surname?'

'No, it's the name I was christened.'

'Were you christened in that church over there?' I pointed to a building in the far distance that had a cross on top.

He shook his head. 'Not in that one, but one very similar.'

'So where did the name Farlan come from?'

'I've never met someone as eternally curious, as you, Lucy.'

'Sorry.'

'It was an observation, not a criticism. Certainly not something you need to apologise for. I like people who wonder about things.'

'Thanks. Perhaps that's why we get on. So, why did you call yourself Farlan?'

'I wanted a name that reflected the close connection I feel to the earth when I'm on Fetlar. Farlan seemed to fit.'

'It suits you. And is this place yours, now your father's gone?' It sounded insensitive.

His laugh was hollow. 'That depends entirely on what my dear Pa has put in his will. It could all be mine or it could all have been left to a dog charity. Knowing Pa, it will be somewhere in between and will be decidedly underhand.'

There was a knock at the door and a woman walked in. 'Excuse me, Mr Alex, I didn't know you were in here.'

'Mrs Mac, it's lovely to see you.' He gave her a bear hug. 'This is my friend, Lucy. I've dragged her here at a moment's notice and she's got nothing to wear that's suitable for tomorrow's event. Can you sort something out?'

'Why of course. Very nice to meet you, Miss Lucy.' She nodded.

'Sorry if I'm putting you to any trouble.'

'I'll leave you ladies to it.' Farlan disappeared almost as quickly as his foxy friend.

'Do you have anything in mind?' she asked.

'I'm entirely in your hands. Just a black dress, I guess, that's suitable for a funeral. Have you got some old clothes hanging around?'

'There's a selection of clothing that has been around for a while. Mr Sutherland had a strict dress code for dinner and some guests were caught out. I can alter something we already have in. It won't take me long.' She busied herself with a tape measure for a few minutes, taking down my vital statistics. It was embarrassing to hear them being said out loud. I couldn't blame the brandy and chocolate from the day before. It was months of eating the wrong things and not getting enough exercise that had caused it. Well, I'd caused it, by being lazy and indulgent. I remembered James's comment about my thighs. Bastard. He was wrong to have said it but he was right. I needed to get a grip. At least it had been a good day today, foodwise. It was dinner time now and we'd barely eaten.

Fifteen minutes later, Mrs Mac reappeared with a lilac and cream patterned dress and some shoes. There were some tights too. 'I thought you might want something to change into for dinner. This should fit you well enough.'

'That's kind, thank you.' Oh, so there was dinner.

'You'll hear the gong in about twenty minutes. It'll be a light supper, nothing too formal, but there are some other guests dining tonight.'

'Really? Who?' I felt decidedly uncomfortable at the prospect.

'Some cousins of Mr Alex and some of the senior estate staff. I'll leave you to freshen up. I've left some toiletries next door in case you need anything.'

I dashed into the bathroom and felt a wave of anxiety wash over me. I thought Farlan and I would have a quiet night in, maybe a microwave meal or takeaway pizza in front of the TV in his parents' house. Instead, I was in a grand country house, in a borrowed dress, with a group of people who were used to these surroundings. Farlan, or rather Alex, who would be busy chatting away to everyone, oozing charisma and confidence in his new role as Lord of the Manor, or Laird or whatever it was. I looked in the mirror. Please don't let me make a fool of myself. I had a quick wash, put on some fresh deodorant and make-up, all the while praying the dress Mrs Mac had brought me wouldn't make me look like a fat lump.

I went back to my room and closed my eyes as I put the dress over my head. I had a quick peek. It was actually OK. In fact, I looked quite nice. It had a V-neck and some ruching at the waist, which made it flattering to my shape. The shoes were a bit tight but better that than have them dropping off my feet. I did not want to start the evening by falling down that grand staircase in front of upper-class strangers.

I put on some extra lip salve in an effort to make my dry lips look a bit glossy then stood back to look in the mirror. Not bad. I winked at myself then heard the gong. Showtime.

I waited a minute, took a breath then walked out into the corridor. Farlan was walking along the opposite corridor. He had trimmed his beard and was wearing a casual suit, if there is such a thing. It was like looking at a different person to the one I knew from the cottage.

He gave me a broad smile and walked towards me as I made my way to the top of the staircase. 'Why, Miss Lucy. You look lovely.' He took my arm and held on to me tightly as we made our way down the stairs.

'So do you, Alex. Will it matter if I forget and call you Farlan?'

'Not at all.'

Chapter 12

From the bottom of the stairs, Farlan and I walked across the hallway to the dining room. There was a hubbub of conversation that stilled as we approached the entrance. 'Alexander, wonderful to see you.' 'Alex, you old dog.' 'Xander, where have you been?' the voices said.

He began talking to people and I tried to melt into the background. It struck me as odd that no-one offered condolences to him, but perhaps they'd already done that.

A tall, thin man in a charcoal suit, who I guessed to be in his fifties, offered his hand to me. 'I'm Jonty, I don't think I've had the pleasure.' His eyes sparkled.

'Lucy. I'm...a friend of er, Alex's.'

'Lovely to meet you. How's he doing?'

'Very well, under the circumstances.' I didn't feel in any position to comment. 'Are you a member of the family?'

'I'm the family solicitor but also a cousin. I'm pleased he's here at all. I got the impression when I spoke to him that he wasn't going to return from his hermit lifestyle.'

I wasn't sure what to say, worried that he wanted information from me that Farlan wouldn't want me to share. 'I suppose grief hits everyone differently.'

'Huh. If there's any grief at all, given the animosity he felt towards Struan, but I suppose there was always emotion between them, however bad. It's indifference that would have kept him away, not hatred. Would you excuse me?'

He disappeared off to talk to a willowy woman with long, dark hair who reminded me of Morticia Addams. I felt the hint of a smile cross my lips at my catty thought but stifled it, given the occasion, though when I looked around the room, no-one seemed to be overtly sad. It was probably just another house party to this lot. I tried not to look like a wallflower but didn't fancy wandering up to one of the cliques and trying to join their conversation.

'Darling, what a lovely dress.' A blonde with a generous chest and tiny waist touched my arm.

'I'm afraid I don't know its provenance. I've had to borrow it. I wasn't expecting any of this,' I put on my best posh voice and gestured around the room.

'Xander is a naughty boy. He should have warned you about us all. I'm Letitia. One of the family.'

'Nice to meet you, Letitia.'

'Call me Tish. How long have you known my dashing cousin?'

I wondered if I should let on. 'Not long.'

'And yet he brings you here. Is he smitten?' She was fishing for information, there was no doubt in my mind.

'Well, you know Xander, Tish. It's hard to tell.'

She let out a giggle that sounded false. 'So true. We promised ourselves to each other if we hit forty and weren't married. Only two years to go.' She sounded hopeful.

'Never mind.' My comment made her narrow her eyes in my direction. 'Do you live close by?'

'I only pop up here for the occasional event. Mostly I keep myself amused in London.' She poked half-heartedly at the olive in her martini with a cocktail stick.

I was drinkless but that was probably a good thing. I certainly wanted to keep my wits about me in this alien crowd. 'And what do you do in London?'

'A little modelling. I'm working on my media career at the moment.' She finally speared the olive and ate it, barely chewing.

'Well, good luck with that.' I felt guilty as I didn't mean it.

'What about you? It's Lucy, isn't it?'

'I'm writing a book at the moment. Spending time with Xander is helping me with that.' I was starting to enjoy myself, putting on this false persona of a confident woman of independent means.

'Good for you.' She patted my hand in a patronising gesture. 'I thought about writing a book. One has so many ideas but it's committing the time to writing them down, isn't it?'

'Oh, yes. Anyone can write a book if they can be bothered.' I knew I was talking as much horseshit as she was.

'Xander!' she squealed, as Farlan came towards us. She gave him a long hug and stroked his left buttock in what seemed like a show of possession.

He extricated himself from her hold. 'Tish, you've obviously met Lucy.' He spoke to me directly. 'Are you alright?'

'Of course, I'm alright, darling.' My voice sounded like an exaggerated plummier version of Tish's.

He looked at me oddly. 'Have you er…had a drink?'

'No, no-one's offered me anything at all. But I'm fine. You go and mingle.' I winked at him and he frowned before moving swiftly to the opposite side of the room. He obviously thought I was half-cut, not realising I was trying to keep myself afloat in this introvert's nightmare by pretending a little. I felt a wave of relief when the gong sounded again and people went to sit down. They all seemed to know where to go so I waited until they'd all claimed a seat then made for the empty one. I was miles away from Farlan but I was sitting between Jonty and his father, Alasdair, who it turned out had been the family solicitor till he retired a few years back. Alasdair, luckily, had enough manners to set me at my ease and not ask too many awkward questions. He chatted away, telling me anodyne tales of the family. The evening passed by pleasantly enough and the food was lovely. Once pudding had been served, I asked Alasdair to tell me about Struan.

He looked at me for a moment, as if deciding whether to tell the truth or not. 'He was a complex man. Hard to get to know. Had a strict sense of what was right and wrong, and what one's duties were.' He took a nip from a hip flask he took out of his jacket's inside pocket.

I shook my head when he offered the flask to me. 'No, thank you. Was it the duty aspect that made him and Alexander fall out?'

He gave the question genuine thought. 'That was certainly a part of it, but mainly it came from Xander not being able to forgive his father for sending him away to school. Struan thought it would be the making of him, but to do it when his mother had just died was hard for Xander to take. And then the beatings, of course. In reality,

I think every argument they had boiled down to Xander feeling abandoned to that draconian educational regime and Struan feeling Xander had let him down.'

'How did he let Struan down?' I couldn't help but ask.

'For not taking his punishment like a man. For running away. To Struan that was dereliction of duty.'

'How old was Xander?'

'Eight or nine, maybe. In today's world, you'd say Struan was entirely at fault but it's unfair to blame him, when he was from a different era.'

I'd been so caught up in the conversation, I hadn't noticed Farlan come over to our side of the table.

'Alasdair, I do hope you're not giving away all my secrets.' He said it politely yet there was a steely tone to his voice.

'Indeed, I rather thought this young lady knew them already.'

I was sure he didn't remember my name but he was in his early eighties, so he was entitled to be forgetful. 'Alasdair's been very gallant, looking after me in this sea of strangers.' I smiled at Farlan but he didn't meet my gaze.

He looked at his watch then addressed the room. 'Gentlemen, if you'd like to join me in the billiard room, we can leave the ladies to their gossip.'

Did people still live like this? It's 2023, I wanted to shout, not 1923. But they all seemed quite happy to carry on as though they were dining at *Gosford Park*, so I waited till the men had gone, to see how many women were left. There were seven of us. Well, there were six of them and me. They talked about people, places and events that meant nothing to me, so I excused myself and walked upstairs to the bathroom next to my bedroom. I looked in the shaving mirror and could see a smudge of mascara had strayed onto my temple so I cleaned it up and went to my room to check my full-length reflection. I looked awful. The dress was creased and my hair was messy. My pseudo-confidence bubble deflated. Feeling a complete social failure, I decided to stay in my room. No-one would miss me. I opened my bag and found the copy of *Emma* I'd been reading in the library the previous day. I wished I was back there. I couldn't see that my presence here was helping Farlan at all. He'd seemed quite grumpy with me all evening. I took off my shoes, rubbed my sore toes and sat up on the bed. The pillows were lovely and soft, deep and chock-full of feathers. I sat back and got comfortable then turned to where I'd stopped reading.

I'd lost myself completely in Highbury with *Emma* and had got to the point where Mr Knightley was telling Emma off for being horrible to Miss Bates, when the door of my room opened, startling me.

'Here you are. Everyone said you'd disappeared.' Farlan looked concerned. 'Are you feeling alright?'

I nodded. 'I'm sorry. I tried my best to be sparkly and entertaining but I'm not good with new people and I ran out of confidence.' I turned my palms up to emphasise the point.

He took my hands and pulled them together between his. 'You've nothing to prove here, not to these people. It's been good to have you with me, particularly on the journey. I'd have turned around a hundred times if you hadn't been by my side.'

'Does that mean you want me to leave now?'

He shook his head. 'Not at all. Tonight is all about catching up with my old life but tomorrow's going to be the tough part. Knowing I've an ally in the room, someone who knows Farlan, not Alex, will help me get through the day, if you don't mind staying.'

'Not at all. Do you need me to come back downstairs and be sociable?' I crossed my fingers in the hope he didn't.

'You're fine. Enjoy the rest of *Emma*. You looked lovely tonight.' He bent down and kissed me gently on the forehead before leaving.

I got up and locked the door, wanting to know I could get undressed and go to sleep without fear of anyone coming into the room by accident. The curtains didn't quite meet and there was a crescent moon, which bathed the front of the house in soft light.

I woke up a few minutes after 3am, disturbed by a noise outside. At first, I thought it was a woman screaming, but as I came to and tuned into it, I recognised it as a fox's bark. I got up and looked out. The moon was obscured by wispy clouds, but there was enough light to make out the shape of an animal on the front lawn. It was Mr Fox. As I pulled the curtains open wider, it turned around and its eyes glinted in the moonlight and fixed on me. Did it want me to go to it? A voice pierced the gloom and shouted, "Get off with ya," and a shot rang out. The fox ran off into the hedge and away from danger. The same voice shouted "Bloody vermin" and a door slammed shut somewhere below me.

I wanted to check that Farlan was alright but I worried I'd go to the wrong room and disturb a stranger, so I stayed where I was.

Chapter 13

It didn't feel like I ever got back to sleep but I was woken at 7:30am by a tap on the door. I got out of bed to unlock it.

'Good morning, Miss Lucy. I've brought you some breakfast. Mr Alex said he thought you'd prefer to eat up here rather than with the other guests.' Mrs Mac put a tray on a small table by a nursing chair and pulled open the curtains. She had done me proud with porridge, toast with butter and marmalade, and some nice strong tea.

'That's kind of you. Thank you.'

'I've your dress here. Do take a moment to try it on and let me know if there's any further alterations needed.' She hung up a black suit carrier.

'Thank you so much. Do you know the timing of everything today?'

'They'll begin the walk down to the kirk at 10:30am for the 11am service. After the interment, there's some drinks and light refreshments back here. And I believe the will is being read at 3pm, though…erm…'

'Oh, no, I won't be part of that, quite right.'

'I've found another pair of shoes, as I wasn't sure if the pair from yesterday were comfortable. These have a lower heel, which will be better for the walk to the kirk. Can I get you anything else?'

'You've been so kind already. I do appreciate your help, Mrs Mac.'

'I've known Mr Alex since he was born. I'd do anything for him.'

I wondered if I dared ask. Sod it, why not? 'So, you must have seen what boarding school and the beatings did to him?'

'Aye, it was terrible, that poor wee laddie being subjected to such harsh punishment time after time.'

'And what happened to make it stop?'

She frowned at me. 'Well, of course it was the hanging incident.' She stopped. 'Och, it's not for me to say. I mustn't speak out of turn.' She backed away towards the door. 'I'll leave you to enjoy your breakfast.' She went out of the room.

The hanging incident? WTAF?

I buttered a piece of toast and thought about what a hanging incident could be. Everything I imagined seemed horrible, so I tried not to think about it as I ate the rest of my breakfast.

The black dress was perfect. It was a simple pattern and was made of quite thick material that kept my bulges under control and looked smart and elegant. The shoes were a much better fit. Mrs Mac came back a few minutes before 10am with a small black fascinator she'd found and helped me fix it in my hair. I had no handbag, so I left everything behind and walked downstairs to see if Farlan was around. It was eerily quiet in the hallway so I looked at the paintings that were on show. They all appeared to be ancestors and I guessed the one nearest the stairs must be Struan. There was such a likeness to Farlan, with the exception of the eyes. Struan's were grey and cold. I was glad I'd not met him.

Slowly, people began to congregate and Tish came over to see where I'd disappeared to the previous night.

'I was tired from all the travelling. Didn't want to make a fuss.'

Jonty came to say hello and Tish moved away. 'The fair Lucy. You kept my father entertained last night, thank you. He was very enamoured.'

'I think he did much more of the entertaining than me. Is he not here?'

'He'll go straight to the kirk. His legs aren't up to the walk.'

Farlan appeared at 10:30am, looking magnificently brooding in black. He nodded his head towards me but was being talked at by several people who all wanted his attention. A small bell tinkled and Farlan led the walk to the kirk. It seemed to be deliberately slow and surprisingly silent, given how talkative this bunch had been the night before. I stayed at the back, trying to be as inconspicuous as possible, so was on the opposite end of the semi-circle to Farlan as we waited outside the kirk for the hearse to arrive.

The body was carried in by pallbearers as a lone piper played then everyone filed in through the sturdy wooden doors. Two men stood either side of the entrance and handed out orders of service and I stood back to let people go in and sit down. Someone nudged me and pointed toward the front pew. Farlan was gesturing to me so I walked up to where he was standing. I hadn't been sure if he'd wanted me to sit with him or just be around but he grabbed my hand and squeezed it tight. The vicar (or minister or whatever they called them in Scotland) told the congregation to sit down. Farlan kept my hand in his.

I could tell when he found parts of the service difficult because he'd grip my hand more tightly. When it came time for the eulogy, Farlan stood up and began to read from the sheet in front of him, but when he got to the part about his mother and her death, he started to struggle and there was an awkward silence. I waited for someone to do something, for one of his cousins or friends to step up, but no-one did. It was a tumbleweed moment. I looked around and everyone else seemed to be staring either at the floor or at Farlan with embarrassment. Without thinking whether it was the right thing to do, I went to stand next to him, found the place he'd got up to in his speech and carried on reading it. I felt so protective of him in that moment that speaking on his behalf came naturally. I found my voice was confident and clear as I finished the tribute to a man I hated, despite never having met him.

Farlan had regained his composure by the time I finished reading and we sat back down on the front pew. There was a hymn next, which gave me some time to deal with the sudden wobble in my legs from what I'd done. I hated public speaking with a passion, but I'd been overtaken by compassion for Farlan and thank goodness, hadn't made a mess of it or a fool of myself.

'Thank you,' Farlan whispered in my ear as the hymn finished and it was my turn to squeeze his hand. The service finished shortly afterwards and I walked with Farlan behind the coffin out to the gravesite. I mentally tuned out for the interment, still wondering what a hanging had to do with anything that had gone on between Farlan and his father.

When we returned to the house, the drinks reception was muted, out of respect, with none of the braying laughter there'd been the night before. There were canapés being passed around on silver trays but I'd no appetite. I know I spoke to a few people but the conversations were forgettable and my mind was elsewhere. In truth, I was watching Farlan, because I knew the next part of the day was the one that was causing him most anxiety.

Jonty tapped a teaspoon against his champagne flute to get everyone's attention as a clock struck 3pm. 'Can all those invited to the will reading please make their way to the library?'

Farlan pulled me to one side. 'It's likely we'll be leaving as soon as this is over, so can you make sure your bag is packed?' He said it quietly, so only I could hear.

I nodded and left the room to go upstairs. I wasn't sure if I should change out of the dress and leave it behind. I went downstairs to see if I could find Mrs Mac, but apart from the guests who weren't at the will-reading, there seemed to be no-one around. I decided to keep the dress on and travel in it, at least for the first part of the journey. I didn't fancy people seeing me leave in the tattered jeans and worn fleece I'd arrived in. I took off the fascinator and left it on the side table.

I sat in my bedroom, looking out towards the kirk where Struan's body had been buried and tried to imagine my life back in Croydon. So much had happened in such a short time and I felt as though my confusion about what I wanted from life was beginning to clear. I didn't know the answers yet, but the fog was lifting.

'Lucy!' Farlan's voice echoed up the stairs.

I picked up my bag and opened the door.

Farlan was bounding up the stairs. 'We're leaving. Are you ready?'

I nodded and he dashed into the room directly opposite mine, appearing a few seconds later with his own bag.

I closed the bedroom door and headed down the stairs.

Mrs Mac appeared. 'Safe journey, Miss Lucy.'

'Thank you for all your help. Am I OK to take this with me?' I put my hands on the dress.

'Aye, I think the dress code will be more relaxed in future, so you may as well take it, if you can get some use out of it.' She looked at me with a warm smile then turned her gaze on Farlan. 'Goodbye, Mr Alex.'

He gave her the briefest of silent hugs then walked out to the car, where McDonald was waiting with the door open. I put my bag in the back then got in. I'd not got my seatbelt on before Farlan began to speed up the driveway, spitting gravel at all angles.

Chapter 14

Farlan was clearly annoyed, angry or both at the contents of the will reading but I decided to sit quietly and wait for him to say something before venturing any conversation.

'We're not booked on flights till tomorrow morning so we'll get a room near the airport tonight.'

'OK.' I waited for him to say something else but he was mute for the rest of the journey. I tried to enjoy the passing scenery but Farlan's low mood filled the vehicle.

He pulled up at a hotel after an hour of too-fast driving. 'Wait there.' He went in, I assumed, to enquire about rooms. He came out a few minutes later and moved the car into the main car park. We took our bags into reception and I looked longingly at the vending machine. I'd not eaten since breakfast and my stomach was rumbling.

'Lucy! This way.'

I followed him up a flight of stairs to a room.

'Sorry, but they only have the one room. It is a twin though. Is that OK? I can sleep in the car if not.'

I looked at him and could see he was shattered, probably more mentally than physically. 'It's fine. Absolutely fine.' I tried to lighten the mood a little. 'Bags I the best bed though.'

He opened the door. It wasn't as nice a room as the one I'd woken up in, but it was pleasant enough and the bedding looked spotless.

'Take your pick,' he said.

I chose the one nearest the bathroom and sat on it, putting my bag at the end.

'Are you hungry?' he asked.

'Was it that obvious?'

'You were drooling at the sight of the vending machine, so yes, fairly obvious.' He smiled and it was lovely to see, after everything that had happened.

'Sorry. Didn't eat any lunch.'

'Me neither. Just as well, I'd probably have thrown up over Jonty if I had. There is a restaurant here. It's not Michelin but it looks OK. We can eat when it opens.'

'If you're sure. I'm quite happy to raid the vending machine and the mini-bar if you don't want to deal with people.'

'Are you obsessed with brandy and chocolate?' A smile played on his lips.

'I'm only thinking of you. You don't want to be around people.'

'Oh, right.' He laughed. 'I'm fine with people. It's just some people I wanted to get away from.'

'Do you want to talk about it?' I hoped he did.

'Not much to say. My father did exactly what I expected him to do.'

'Which was what?'

'Try and manipulate me into being what he wanted me to be.'

'How?'

'By putting in his will that the entire estate is left to me, but only if I live there and run it until I'm sixty years old. If I don't agree to that or if I stop running it before I reach sixty, the estate is sold and the proceeds divided up between the cousins. And I get nothing.'

'Jeez, what a wanker.' I spoke without thinking. 'What does he mean, run the estate? What else is there apart from the house and garden?'

He gave me an odd look. 'The estate's 12,000 acres.'

I hadn't a clue how big that was but was sure I'd read Windsor Great Park was about 5,000 acres. 'What are your responsibilities as estate owner?'

'It all needs to be managed, the rivers, the loch, the hills and the heather, the wildlife. There are four species of deer, eagles, grouse and kestrels to consider. There's self-catering accommodation and the estate workers' cottages and other buildings, like the stables, to maintain. And, of course, that money pit of a house. He wanted me to take over from him, but I was set on going to medical school. When I decided to specialise in psychiatry, he hated me even more for not wanting to be the next Laird. This is his way of forcing me to take it on, by leaving me nothing if I won't. He was a control freak and he's still trying to get me to do his bidding, from beyond the grave.'

'But you don't need the money, do you? You said you've got money from an inheritance. Or was it a house? But you've some way to support yourself.'

'That wasn't strictly true. I was getting a small allowance from a trust fund that Pa had set up way back, but that will stop now. I need to decide what to do next. I mean, I can go back to psychiatry.

I can go back to London and earn plenty. But I enjoy being Farlan way more than I ever liked being Dr Sutherland.'

'When do you need to decide?'

'I've got a week. I have to let Jonty know my intention a week today otherwise he'll put the estate on the market.'

'Can't he give you more time? He seemed like a decent chap.'

'He's one of the beneficiaries if I don't agree to run the estate, so he won't be hanging around with the sale. The others wouldn't let him. Sorry. This must all be very boring for you.'

'Are you kidding? This is one of the most interesting things that's ever happened to me.' I stopped myself. 'Sorry, that sounds insensitive, like I'm seeing your life as entertainment. This is all so outside my sphere of normal existence that I'm fascinated by it. But that is completely unimportant. The whole point of me coming with you is to be here for you, to help you if I can. Try and support you in any way possible.'

'You don't have to do that.'

'I absolutely do, because you've already helped me. And you've helped lots of other people, too. It's time someone returned the favour.'

'How have I helped you?'

'You've got me away from my dull, destructive life. Thanks to you, I now realise how unhappy I was. I don't think I'd have ever left if you hadn't helped me see it for what it was.'

'Thanks. I'm glad for you.'

'Now, I've got to work out what it is I want to do with my life.'

'You can do anything you like, Lucy. Whatever makes you happy.'

'The same goes for you, Farlan.' I met his gaze.

He gave a flat smile. 'I suppose it does. Thank you.'

After an average dinner in the hotel's restaurant, Farlan and I sat in the bar for an hour, having a post-meal liqueur and talking about books. He had read way more than me so I wasn't sure I kept my end of the conversation up. We started discussing Shakespeare plays and Dickens novels, which was fine, but he recommended Jean-Paul Sartre after I'd talked about Jilly Cooper. But literature was a safe topic and that was definitely all he was in the mood for.

We flew back to Sumburgh the next morning then did some shopping on the way to the first ferry. The weather had settled so the ferry crossings weren't too bumpy. We carried some of the shopping back to the cottage, with the expectation we'd pick up the rest in the morning. Farlan heated up some chilli from a tin and we ate it with tortilla chips and grated cheese as an early dinner. He lit the fire and we sat in front of it, post-food, both tired from the journey.

I poured him a whisky and found the bottle of brandy I'd been guzzling in the library. There was a bit left so I poured some into a crystal tumbler. With the glow of the fire and the mellow warmth from the brandy, I decided I would ask him the question I'd been curious to hear the answer to. 'Can I ask you something?'

'Sure, though I can't promise I'll answer it.' He took a sip of whisky. 'And as long as you're not asking me about my decision on the will.'

'Not that.' I hesitated.

'What then?'

'I heard about the hanging incident. Was it revenge for something? Who was hanged? Will you tell me what happened?'

His face clouded. 'No.'

'So, there are secrets here?'

He shook his head. 'Don't. Just don't.' And I could tell from the tension in his shoulders that the subject was closed.

'Sorry, I shouldn't have asked. I was being selfish. It's none of my business.' I took a sip of brandy. 'It's good to be back here.' I was keen to change the subject.

'Is it? Don't you find it a little spartan?'

'I guess. But the atmosphere is peaceful, almost otherworldly. I feel so calm in myself. I've been trying to work out what it is. It's the lack of stressful situations. I was always on edge before I came here. Probably been overdosing on cortisol my whole adult life. Here is bliss in comparison. Though I do have to get used to having porridge for breakfast every morning.'

'I've probably overcompensated on the simple life with how I've got everything here. I was trying to put as much distance between myself and my old life as I could. I could put in a proper stove, sort out better heating, get Wi-Fi rigged up even. But I wanted to get away from civilisation.'

'You succeeded pretty well in that regard. But you've no money coming in now, so how will you afford it? If you were to stay and not live on the estate, I mean. If you are going to take on the estate management, it doesn't matter, does it? You'll be going from here and that'll be that. I suppose you could run a retreat on the estate, do your good works there, instead of here. You said there were self-catering places?'

'Let's not talk about it.'

'Sorry, was thinking out loud. Something else I meant to ask you.'

An expression of annoyance flashed across his face. 'What?'

'Someone at the shop said something about people leaving here mostly happy, but there being the odd woman who'd gone home disappointed. What did you do to disappoint them?'

He looked at me and a hint of a smile played on his lips. 'It was more what I didn't do. I didn't fall in love with them and ask them to stay forever.'

'Blimey. I mean, I get that you're irresistible to all women but would they really have wanted to live up here?' I bit the inside of my lip to stop myself laughing.

'Irresistible, eh? I'll take that, even though you've insulted my beautiful home.'

'I'm very sorry but it's probably a step too far from London living.' I yawned. 'I'm going to have an early night, if you don't mind. I had to share a room with a snorer last night and didn't get a lot of sleep.'

'You've got some nerve. I don't snore any more than you do.'

'Whatever you say, Farlan.' I gave him a brief hug and a peck on the cheek. 'Goodnight. If you need to talk, anytime, you know where I am.'

I went to the bathroom to brush my teeth and decided I should probably give James a call in the morning. Or maybe I'd text him now. I sat up in bed and sent a "Hi. How are you doing?" message.

He rang straight back. 'Are you OK?'

'Yeah. Just going to bed. Thought I'd check in with you. Did you check your passport expiry?'

'It's got a year to run. What have you been up to on your course?'

'Reading. Writing. Thinking.'

'Sounds deadly. As long as you're enjoying yourself.'

I opened my mouth to tell him how wonderful the island was but stopped. He wouldn't get it. He wouldn't think it was wonderful. I didn't actually want him here anyway.

'Are you missing me at all, Luce?'

'Probably about as much as you're missing me.'

'Oh. You're in one of those moods. I'll leave you to it. Night.'

'Night, James.' I was going to say "Love you" out of habit but the words didn't appear.

'Don't go silly up there, will you Luce? Like you did last year.'

I could feel myself blushing.

'Thanks for bringing that up. Night, James.' I ended the call.

A year ago, I'd had a mental fling with someone at work. I called it a mental fling because it was only in my head. I'd developed a crush on this guy. We'd been working late together on a shitty project and I misread the signals. James had sensed something was up before anything started, but his interrogation about it had made me feel guilty for even thinking things. I felt blindsided by the accusations and he'd assumed my confusion was guilt, almost delighting in it. It had been a difficult time but we'd weathered the storm. Although a better description was that James was the storm and I'd weathered his trial by shouting, feeling grateful to have done so. My crush moved to a new department at the end of the project and suddenly, life was back to normal. Except it wasn't.

'Night, Lucy,' Farlan shouted through the bedroom door.

'Goodnight.' I suspected it would be anything but.

Chapter 15

When I woke up, I had a vague memory of dreaming about Jenna, about what she'd said of her own struggles and how Farlan had made her realise she was self-abusing. It surprised me. If anything, I'd expected to be haunted by memories of my mental fling. It had bothered me for a long time and now it had resurfaced. I thought I'd be anxious about it again, but maybe the need to explore my own shortcomings was taking precedence and my subconscious was more worried about my behaviour than my thoughts. Was I the same as Jenna? I was in a retreat, with nothing to worry about. I'd stopped the world so I could get off and take stock and what had I done? Drank wine and brandy, and eaten chocolate. I felt annoyed at my behaviour and ashamed too but I knew the sense of disappointment in myself wouldn't stop me doing it again. How could I get myself to act differently?

I tried to make my brain concentrate on finding the answer, thinking hard till my head started to ache, but not even a spark of an idea presented itself. I got up, feeling frustrated and decided, however embarrassed I'd feel about doing it, that I'd bite the bullet and ask Farlan, or rather Doctor Sutherland, for advice.

I found a note stuck on the door of the library that said "Be back in an hour". I paced around the cottage, like an expectant father in a maternity ward. I was impatient to speak to Doctor Sutherland, ask him the questions that had continued to swirl around my head like soap suds in a washing machine.

Farlan arrived back at the cottage a little after 9am with a scowl on his face, grimacing at his phone.

'Oh,' I said.

'What?'

'I wanted to talk to Dr Sutherland but you look like you're distracted.'

His face softened. 'I'm fine.' He took off his coat, put his phone on the side table, took in a deep breath as if to reset his mood and sat down on the sofa.

I felt quite nervous at the prospect of opening up to him. 'Where do you want me?'

He laughed. 'Want you? Do you think I've got a couch set up somewhere? Just sit down and talk to me.'

I felt a bit foolish because of his response and blushed as I sat on the armchair. How many times had I sounded like an idiot to him?

'Do you have to beat yourself up at every opportunity? Stop it.'

'How do you know that's what I was doing?'

'You've a beautifully expressive face. Don't ever try and play poker.' He smiled gently and I sensed he was trying to put me at my ease. 'What do you want to talk about?'

I let out my breath slowly before speaking. 'I'm wondering if you think I self-sabotage, self-abuse like Jenna?'

'Why do you think that you do?'

'Two reasons. Brandy and chocolate. Three, if you include the wine I had at Lorna's place. I kidded myself that my over-indulgence at home was because I was busy and stressed at work, that I didn't have time to be healthy and look after myself, but here

I am, no work, not a thing to do, nothing to worry me, you to take care of me and I'm still being lazy, eating junk food and overdrinking. I don't know how to break the cycle. I'm sure if I can only get started, I'll feel better. But if I can't start here, if left to my own devices, all I do is eat, drink and sit on my fat backside reading books, well, I'm pretty pathetic, aren't I?'

'Are you?' He gazed at me with an intensity that felt as though he was boring into my soul with his deep brown eyes.

I shrug.

'Tell me what your life would be like if you did become the opposite of this pathetic person you claim to be?'

'Perfect Lucy would get up early every morning, go for a run, eat healthy food, not drink alcohol, meditate, do yoga.'

'And do you think you'd want to be friends with this perfect version of yourself?'

I chewed my bottom lip. 'I don't think she'd want to be friends with me, but I'd be in awe of her.'

'Why?'

'To be so in control of herself.'

He nodded. 'Is that your goal then?'

'I guess it is.'

'To be Perfect Lucy who others are in awe of?'

'Someone people aspire to be. Yes.'

'OK.' His tone of voice was firm and clipped. This was Dr Sutherland's voice. 'Tell me about Croydon. What did you write about your life there?'

I felt a squirm of discomfort in my gut. 'I wrote about how unfulfilling it was. How bored I felt with work and home. How I never got the chance to be creative anymore. How easily I'd given up doing the things I loved to be the person I thought James wanted me to be. Even then, he still criticised me for all the ways I wasn't perfect and he was horrible to me, at times. Whatever I did, I couldn't make him stop criticising.'

'So, why did you cry? After you'd written all that down?'

'I felt as though I wasn't good enough and it didn't matter how hard I tried, despite wasting four years of my life trying.'

'And you cried about that?'

'I cried because I could never make him happy. I mean, I could have wasted my entire life trying but I'd still have failed. Ultimately, I'm a failure at relationships. Realising that is what made me cry.' I bit back the emotion I could feel welling up inside me.

'Was James the right person for you?'

'I don't think so. I could never make him happy.'

'Did he make you happy?'

I thought for a while. 'He made me feel wanted.'

'That's not the same thing. Maybe you need to find someone who's prepared to put some effort into making you happy.'

'What's the point? If I couldn't make James happy, with all that effort, why is it going to work with anyone else?' I turned my palms to the ceiling.

Farlan's phone rang. 'Shit, sorry. I need to take this.' He looked at the screen and took the call. 'Hi, Ross. I've been delayed. I'll get a later crossing. Thanks for checking.' He ended the call and put his phone back on the table.

'Sorry, am I keeping you?' I asked.

He shook his head. 'It's fine. This is important.'

'Thanks.' I gave him a smile of gratitude. 'If you're sure.'

He nodded. 'So, you want to be this perfect woman, this healthy athlete who's completely in control of herself. What about this bit of you, the creative person, that you described as lost? Does she fit in with your vision of Perfect Lucy?'

I shook my head. 'Oh no. She's an entirely different version of Perfect Lucy. I mean, they could be one and the same person, but I think that's too much personality to fit in one human. Perfect Lucy would be exhausted.'

'She would indeed.' He laughed.

His laughter hit a nerve. 'Is this a joke to you?'

His face darkened. 'Absolutely not.'

'I feel like you're laughing at me, like you think I'm an idiot. Like the answer to my problems is obvious but I'm too stupid to see it.' I felt quite sick at the thought that what I'd said was true.

'Nothing could be further from the truth. I'll tell you what I think. I think you have self-esteem issues because you don't value yourself in the way you should. I think you treat yourself much more harshly than you'd dare treat anyone else. And you already told me you have a habit of thinking junk food and alcohol can change the way you feel.'

'Can you fix me?' I could hear myself pleading.

'I've said before, Lucy, you're not broken. I want you to listen carefully to what I'm going to say. You're an intelligent and beautiful person who's empathetic, self-aware and caring towards others. Think about how you finished reading the eulogy for me. You're a self-confessed introvert, yet you ignored your discomfort to help me out. What a lovely person that makes you.' He had locked his gaze on me and was watching my expression.

I could see he was getting annoyed.

'I see that look on your face. Shaking your head because you're too polite to openly disagree with me but you're dismissing my words, because they dare to compliment you. You need to accept and believe it when people say nice things about you, because I suspect they do, all the time. You tune them out to fit the narrative in your mind that you're a bad person, unworthy of love and respect. You have to believe what the rest of the world knows. You're a good person, Lucy Brown. You need to turn your brain around, to accept that there's nothing wrong with you. You want to improve some aspects of your life so you can become the best version of yourself and that's to be applauded. I can't snap my fingers, say some magic words and you'll suddenly turn into a different person, the mythical Perfect Lucy. Even if I could, I wouldn't want to. She sounds like a real pain in the arse who'd make everyone around her feel inadequate.'

'But can you help me be a better person?' I gave a flat smile. 'Please?'

He leant forward. 'I'm going to suggest a couple of things if that's OK.'

I nod.

'I want you to read up on some Japanese concepts – Ikigai, Kintsugi and Wabi-sabi.'

'OK.' This sounded a bit weird.

'And I'd like you to think differently about how you tackle changing things in your life.'

'In what way?'

'I think you're hard on yourself too easily. Because every morning, when you don't get up early and go out for a five-mile run, you self-flagellate. And that leads to you feeling down about yourself, and that's the path that draws you towards the wine, brandy and chocolate, which you like at the time but hate afterwards, and then you don't get up the next morning to do a five-mile run because you feel awful after your over-indulgence, so you self-flagellate.'

I nod.

'But, Lucy, doing that early-morning run is the end goal. Think about a small positive step you could take in the direction of that goal. Try and go out for a ten-minute walk before breakfast. And don't say "I must do that every morning." Give yourself a chance to succeed. Set a target of four or five days a week. I bet once you're out, you'll walk for more than ten minutes, because I think you like the mental freedom walking gives you. Start at ten, then do fifteen, then twenty.'

'That sounds like something we do at work. Kaizen.'

'That's exactly what it is.'

'Small incremental steps. Think small, not big.'

'Yes. By all means, have big goals. But don't give yourself grief because you don't reach your goal on Day One.'

'Thanks. I get that.' My mind started to buzz with ideas about how I could use his suggestion.

He looked at his watch. 'I'm sorry, but I'm going to have to get off soon. Hopefully you've a few things to think about.' He got up.

'Plenty, thank you. How long will you be gone?'

'A week or so.'

'A week?' My voice was shrill.

'Are you not comfortable being here on your own?'

'I'm fine with that.'

'So, what's wrong then?'

'Nothing. It's just a surprise you'll be gone that long.'

He looked at me like he didn't believe me.

I didn't believe me either. In truth, I enjoyed his company. It would have been good to have him around while I wrestled with Ikigai, Kintsugi and Wabi-sabi. 'Have you any books about the Japanese stuff?'

'Let me find them.' He disappeared into the library and I wondered how it would feel to be here on my own.

'Here you are.' He handed me three books.

'Thanks.' I looked at the book covers. 'I'll read them while you're away.'

'You're sure it's OK me leaving?'

'It's fine. I assume you're back off to the mainland?'

He nodded and stood up.

'Safe trip.'

'Thanks. And don't forget, Lucy. You're a good person. Don't let your inner critic tell you otherwise, or they'll have me to deal with when I get back.'

'I'll try and remember.' I hoped he meant it when he said he was coming back.

He moved towards me with his arms open and I walked into his enveloping bear hug.

I closed my eyes and breathed in the scent of him. I waited for him to pull away. 'Make sure you take a key with you.'

He frowned. 'You will be here when I get back?' His face was creased with concern.

'I might be out walking. I won't leave the island, well, not unless you abandon me for too long.'

'I won't do that. Ring me if you need anything.'

'I don't have your number.'

He read it out and I tapped it into my mobile. I sent a text to make sure I'd typed it in correctly. The ping from his phone told me I had. He picked it up with his car keys and took one of the house keys from the table by the front door. He smiled at me before leaving.

As he closed the door, I felt a stillness, a sense of peace in the cottage. I sat, looking out of the window at everything and nothing, as my mind tried to take in what Farlan had said to me.

Chapter 16

I decided to visit the shop and buy a few things for me to eat while Farlan was away. I could cook plenty of things on the single ring. I'd never made porridge in my life and didn't fancy trying and failing, but I was too hungry to go to the shop without eating something, so I finished the packet of tortilla chips from the previous night and made a cup of tea. Though we'd done some shopping before we'd returned to Fetlar, most of our purchases were still in Farlan's car which I assumed he'd taken with him to the ferry.

There was a chilly wind outside as I walked to the shop. I was glad to get inside.

The lady behind the counter greeted me. 'Hello. I didn't know you were still around. Are you staying at the retreat again?'

'Yes, I am.' I picked up a basket and trawled around the shop, trying not to pick up every unhealthy item they had, as I thought about my conversation with Farlan. Maybe I'd treat myself to some chocolate. I didn't need to buy any wine. I'd still got the bottles I'd taken to the cottage.

'Are you planning to stay here long?' The shop assistant, Fiona, took my basket from me at the till.

'Do you know, Fiona, I'm not exactly sure. It's a lovely island. I feel very at home here. I wish I could stay for a long time.'

'It's not for everyone. You have to be at home in yourself to be able to enjoy the distance from the rest of the world. That's £18.27.'

I'd spent more than I thought and it made me consider the practicality of the situation. I was on leave from work, so I was still being paid. But I'd have to go back soon if I wanted them to keep paying my salary. The thought of leaving Fetlar made me feel sick and empty; the thought of going back to London even emptier still. But surely this was the same feeling I got as the end of a holiday drew near. I'd wonder whether I could throw in the day job and live in Florida or Vancouver or Portugal. The thought of being able to stay in Fetlar, to read, write and relax in this place, however cold and damp, really appealed. I put my card into the machine and tapped my PIN number dispiritedly.

'That's all gone through. You can take your card out. If you are going to be around a while, might you consider working here? You'd be great at it. I've heard you in here, talking to other customers. You've just the right personality for it.'

'Me working in the shop? Doing what?'

'Opening up in the morning, manning the till, closing it at the end of the day. Being around when the deliveries come in, stocking the shelves.'

'How come you need someone?'

'One of the ladies who was working here decided to leave. I own the shop with my husband Rory. We live in Lerwick and only pop over when we need to. We'll still be dealing with the orders and the money and everything. We want someone who's here on the island to work alongside the others who look after the café and the Post Office.'

'I might well be interested.' I picked up my now-bulging rucksack and put it on my back.

'Rory will be over here tomorrow. Why don't you come and talk to us both after the shop's closed, say 3pm-ish?'

'I will. Thank you.' I walked out, lost in thought at the idea forming in my head.

As I left, I remembered the island's Interpretive Centre was open, so I went in for a wander around. I found I was getting used to the fact that complete strangers knew my name and my business. It was starting to feel normal.

Chapter 17

I checked out my social media and email accounts the next morning. James had posted something about a promotion on LinkedIn. He'd gone for an interview a while back but hadn't mentioned the outcome, so I hadn't asked. I sent him a WhatsApp message congratulating him and he read it but didn't respond.

My friend Ali had sent me a "Where are you?" message, so I tried to call her.

She didn't pick up but rang back after a few minutes. 'Sorry, was in a middle of changing a poopy nappy. Where are you?'

'One of the Shetland Islands.'

'What the hell are you doing up there?'

I wondered how much to tell her. 'I'm on retreat.' I decided not to tell her much at all.

'I was visiting the in-laws so we called at yours as a surprise last night.'

'Was James there?'

'No. House was empty.'

'He'll have been at the pub or at work. Sorry I missed you.'

'When are you back?'

'Not decided yet.'

'Are you screwing up the courage to leave James?'

'What makes you say that?'

'Nothing in particular. Just a feeling.'

'I don't know what to say. This trip's more about me thinking about myself. I've not finished thinking yet, so anything's possible.'

A wail muffled her words. 'Sorry, I need to do a feed. Call if you want to talk.' I sensed Ali was annoyed with me but maybe she was jealous of the peace and quiet of my location.

Fiona and her husband Rory were very direct in their manner. They explained the shop opening hours for winter and summer, the duties over and above serving customers, which included placing special orders, filling the shelves and taking out of date food off sale. They told me about the other people who worked there. They explained some of the issues that might happen and how they dealt with them. They showed me the old but serviceable laptop in the small room at the back, where I could enter any special orders. They told me the wage, which was small, but then there wasn't anywhere to spend money on the island other than the shop, so it should be enough to live on. I'd managed to take a break from my Amazon shopping habit and I wondered how much of it had been me trying to fill the void in my life with trinkets and tat. I offered to work at the shop for a couple of days free of charge, to see if they thought I was suitable. They immediately agreed. They didn't ask anything about me, didn't request any references or question my lack of retail experience. I guess there wasn't that much I could steal and where would I go? Everyone knew everything that was going on, so the ferryman would realise if I was doing a runner with their money. The takings wouldn't be that huge anyway. It was hardly Harrods and most people paid by card.

I walked back to the cottage feeling excited at the thought of a new life. By the time Farlan came back, I'd be ready to tell him my plans and to ask if he was prepared to rent his cottage out to me or even sell it to me. I'd some money tucked away from when my parents had died. I'd promised myself it would only be used for a property purchase. It was enough for a deposit on a studio flat in Croydon, but I hoped it might stretch a bit further in Fetlar. Well, I hoped it would buy Farlan's cottage. He'd have no use for it when he took up his role as Laird of the unpronounceable estate, so it would help him if he could sell it quickly. And maybe, he'd come to visit me once in a while. And me him, when I could afford the flight.

Since his departure, Farlan had texted me every morning to check I was OK, but he didn't reveal anything about what he was doing, so I didn't tell him I'd got a job.

I enjoyed the first few days of shop assistant duties. It was nice to see people and to feel I was contributing to the community a bit. There was an added bonus that if food was going beyond its date, I got the early pick of it, so I would be able to live very frugally. On day three, Fiona and Rory agreed to take me on for a month, to give us all a chance to make sure it was right. I enjoyed the short working day, which gave me plenty of time to read and write. I was mainly reading and would spend hours lolling on a chair in the library, devouring whatever book I'd chosen from the shelves. I'd learned a lot about Ikigai, Kintsugi and Wabi-Sabi, and was beginning to understand why Farlan had suggested I find out about them. I could see that I expected myself to be perfect all the time and saw any failure to be perfect as too much of a negative. Banishing that pursuit of perfection, focusing on my abilities and being comfortable in my own skin were not things that would come to me straight away, but I would try, little by little, to get better. I'd celebrate the small steps in the right direction.

I rang Jenna on the evening of day five without Farlan. She didn't pick up my call but I left a message and she rang back after a few minutes.

'Hey, Lucy. Are you still on Fetlar?'

'Yes. I'm alone up here. Farlan's gone to sort out family stuff on the mainland.'

'Is it a bit creepy being up there on your own?'

'Not at all.'

'You're doing OK then?'

'Yes. I wondered how you were doing. Did it help, being up here? Has it made a difference to you? Or have you slipped back into your old ways? Sorry, it probably sounds rude me asking. I wondered if normal life swallows you up again, once you're away from here?'

'It's early days but life is different. It feels as though I've shed a skin. No. It feels like I'm a butterfly now and I was a chrysalis up there. Re-forming into a better shape.'

'That's good then. I'm pleased.'

'What about you?'

'I think I might be turning into a butterfly while I'm here.'

On the morning of day eight without Farlan, I remembered it was my last day's holiday from my job. It felt odd to even be thinking about London life but before I went to the shop, I rang my boss.

'You still away?' Pete asked. 'Where did you end up going?'

'I'm in the north of Scotland.'

'No suntan, then.'

'Definitely not that sort of holiday. More likely to get windburn than sunburn.'

'I'm sorry for all the unsettling emails. I assume that's what you're ringing about.'

'I haven't seen any emails. My work laptop's at home.'

'Oh, well, I'm glad it hasn't spoiled your holiday.'

'What hasn't spoiled my holiday?'

'News of the redundancies.'

'What?' My brain couldn't process the information before I spoke. 'I'm not going to be able to get back for Monday. That's why I'm calling.'

'There's no need to dash back, Luce. The project's pretty much closed down, now that Group have decided not to fund the new venture. So, you can stay a bit longer, if you can afford to.'

'But you're saying I could be made redundant?'

'Yeah. You need to read the emails, Luce. You need to understand the process and the possible outcomes.'

'But what if I wanted to be made redundant? Could you put me at the top of the list to go?' I held my breath as I waited for his response.

'I can put you on the voluntary list, yes. But is that what you want?'

'Yes. I do.'

'That will make the rest of the team love you even more than they do now. We've got to shed two people. Alice has decided to go back to South Africa, so if you go too, everyone else is safe.'

'Win-win then.' Holy moly, this felt like fate was in favour of my dream.

'What are you going to do with yourself?'

'Stay up here for a bit. I can get work in a shop to give me enough money to live on.'

'Alone? What does James say about it all?'

'He doesn't know yet.'

'Oh.'

'I'd appreciate it if you don't contact him in the next day or so, Pete. I'm planning to speak to him later today.' I'd rather not have to speak to him at all, if I was honest but I knew I had to. I owed him that much.

'OK. Make sure you do, though Luce. Don't let him find out another way.'

'I will. Do I have to do anything about the redundancy request? Email you or fill in something to make this official?'

'There's a form in your inbox. Complete that and send it back then we can start the process. I'll get in touch with HR now, tell them your intention and they'll do a forecast of your final settlement. I can send that across so you'll have an idea of what you might get.'

'Thanks. Will I need to come back to the office at all?'

'Only to bring back your laptop and phone.'

That would be difficult to organise. But not impossible. 'OK. I'll have to see if James will help with that. Listen, thanks. I'll send the email later on today.'

'Cheers, Luce.'

'Thanks, Pete.'

I ended the call and stared at the phone, not quite believing what had happened. I was excited and pleased with myself that I'd acted decisively.

Once I'd closed the shop that afternoon, I went into the back office and used the shop laptop to log into my work emails online. I found the message with the form to be filled in and completed it as best I could. I sent it back to HR, copying Pete. A few minutes later, Pete responded with the details from HR of the potential settlement. I'd only been with the company six years but it wasn't an ungenerous amount. The money would last quite a while on Fetlar and would supplement my shop income. I smiled to myself. It was all starting to come together.

I was about to lock up the shop and walk back to the cottage when I told myself I had to ring James. The phone signal was better here than at the cottage and, for some reason, I didn't want the conversation sullying the atmosphere in what I hoped would be my new home. I pressed the call button.

He answered quickly. 'Lucy.'

'James.'

'Hi. When are you coming back?'

I decided to ignore the question. I wasn't ready to answer that straight away. 'How are you?'

'I'm fine. Any reason I shouldn't be?'

'No. Just checking.' There was an uncomfortable silence.

'Have you finished your course?'

'It wasn't exactly a course. I've been on retreat.'

'OK, whatever. So? When are you coming back?'

'I don't think I am, James. I think I'm going to stay here.'

'What? Where is "here" exactly?'

'It's one of the islands of Shetland.'

'Jimmy Perez-land?'

'Yeah.' His reference to the leading character in a television show jolted me, reminding me of sitting in our cosy front room watching TV together.

'How can you stay up there? What about your job? How are you going to live?' There was an exasperated tone in his voice, as though he was talking to a naughty child.

'I'm being made redundant.'

He didn't respond straightaway and I fought my instinct to fill the silence.

'Right. Have you met someone up there? Is that what this is about? You being silly again? Who is it? Some hippy on this course?'

'No, it's nothing like that. The only person I've met is the real me, who I've decided is happier here.'

'Spare me the New Age wanky bollocks. All that "You've fallen in love with yourself, you've found yourself" shit. You're so gullible, Luce. How much money have they squeezed out of you?'

If I ever needed affirmation that I was doing the right thing, there it was. 'Actually, the retreat was free. And maybe I am gullible. But I quite like me, it turns out. I know I was a constant disappointment to you, because you never hid it. You always criticised me. I can't imagine you'll be that bothered whether I come back or not.'

There was a silence and I thought we'd been cut off. 'James?'

'I'm not going to lie to make you feel better, Luce. Of course, I want you to come back. I'm sorry you saw my helpful suggestions to better yourself as criticism. I'll stop doing that, if that's what you want. Is this a way of getting me to behave better, you threatening not to come home?'

'No, it's not, because I'm not coming back. I suppose I hoped you wouldn't be bothered either way.'

'Lucy-loo, we've been together for what, four-and-a-half years? Do you think I'm that much of a cold-hearted bastard that I wouldn't care if you left? Of course I'm not. But I'm not going to beg you to come home. You need to get this whatever-it-is out of your system. Take as long as you need. I'll be here.'

I wondered what to say. Even if Fetlar didn't work out for me, I knew I didn't want to go back to Croydon or to James. 'I don't want to lie, James. I've no intention of coming back.'

'Don't be silly, Luce. You've had a couple of weeks of them bending your head. You're feeling all spaced out and Zen, and you think you want to stay up there, in the arse end of the country, sniffing incense and meditating. But it'll pass, I know it. And you know it, deep down. So, I'm not going to get all high-handed. I'm telling you I'll wait. I'll give you till Christmas to come to your senses.' His arrogance was breath-taking at times. 'I bet there's a bloke up there, at this retreat, isn't there? Someone who works there or is a fellow inmate? Someone who you get all excited about when he smiles at you?'

I was so tempted to end the call but I still needed him to do something for me. 'The only bloke up here is a psychiatrist.'

'Do you mean psychologist?'

'No. I do understand the difference, James.' I pressed the mute button and let out a scream that sounded like the word fuck. 'Whatever, James, maybe you're right and I will change my mind. But the one thing that is definitely happening is that I am losing my job.'

'That's shitty timing.'

It was perfect timing from my perspective. 'I have to return my laptop and mobile. Would you take them to the office or to Pete's? They're in the spare room, all packed up in my laptop bag.' I don't know why I'd packed everything away neatly before I left. A premonition? Wishful thinking, probably.

'I'll get Pete to meet me at the pub. I haven't seen him for a while. He can buy me a beer as consolation for him getting rid of your job.'

I'd need to ask Pete not to reveal that the choice had been mine. 'Thanks. I appreciate that.'

'I'm not a bad person, Luce.'

'I know.' Not bad, no. Thoughtless, hurtful and selfish at times. But not bad.

'Right. Well, ring me when you change your mind. Bye.' He ended the call.

I stared at the phone for a while. I felt a niggle of guilt but mainly relief that I'd told him. I sent a text to Pete to explain about the laptop. I decided not to ask him to lie to James about me choosing to leave my job. Perhaps it would make James realise I was serious about the move.

As I walked back to the cottage, I tried to think if there was anything in Croydon that I wanted to keep hold of but I couldn't think of a single thing. Sarah had taken all the family photos off me as research material for the eulogy and everything else I possessed was just stuff. It was quite sad that I hadn't left any kind of footprint behind in Croydon. But it did make moving easier.

I felt unsettled when I got back to the cottage but I wasn't sure why. I wasn't afraid of being in the cottage on my own. Fetlar had never felt like a frightening place to me but something wasn't right. Maybe it was that Farlan had been gone too long. I hoped he wasn't having a tough time of it, adjusting to the idea of being the Laird. I hated that I wasn't getting the chance to talk to him, to help him chew over the decisions he was having to make. But maybe that was what was getting to me. That he was settling into his new life and wouldn't even bother returning here. It wasn't that I was unhappy to be here alone, but I felt sad at not being able to say goodbye to Farlan, before he was lost forever and Alex, Laird of the unpronounceable estate, took back the reins of his life. I went to bed, feeling tired but out of sorts.

I decided to get up and make a cup of tea when I'd looked at my phone for the hundredth time to see the clock. It was half-past midnight. I could see a bit of the moon as I peered out of one of the curtains in the main room. The kettle eventually boiled and I made some tea before sitting on the sofa, with the curtain open to give me some moonlight to see by.

As I sipped my tea, I sensed movement in my peripheral vision. I didn't have to look twice to know it was the fox. The flash of its eyes as it stared at the twitching curtain, then the long stare directly into my soul, reminded me of our first encounter. I knew I had to go to it but I was afraid. What if it disappeared and this time left a key for somewhere else? I was scared at the thought that fate didn't want me to stay in Fetlar. Better to know, I decided. And who says I have to take a nudge from fate? Just because it offers me a change, doesn't mean I have to take it, I told myself.

I snapped on the light, went to the door, slipped my coat over my t-shirt and put on my trainers. I turned the key in the lock and could see it was dark out there because the moon had been swallowed by cloud. I left the light on and the door ajar as I walked slowly into the gloom. It took me a while to see the fox. It was staring at me, only a few yards from where I was standing, so I moved slowly towards it. It didn't back away. I moved a step closer and it stood its ground. I decided to sit down and ignored the dampness, putting out my hand to see if the fox would come to me. Warily, it came closer. It sniffed my hand and I could feel its soft breath tickle my fingers. It came forward so my hand was above its head and I stroked it as though it was a dog. I scratched the top of its head and it made a contented guttural noise as I moved my hand under its chin and began to rub, on the sweet spot between chest and chin. Its eyes were closed from the pleasure of the attention. An idea came to mind and I acted on it without thinking. I looked at the fox and whispered into its ear. 'Bite me, Farlan. Bite me.'

I stopped scratching and held my hand in front of its mouth. It moved its head back, sniffed the edge and then clamped its jaw over my hand. I let out a squeak of pain. The bite had broken the skin on my palm and the back of my hand. The fox let go its grip and vanished, as it had in Croydon. I wondered if I'd done the right thing.

I got up and went inside to check the wound. The bite wasn't too bad. I didn't need plasters for the puncture wounds but I was glad I'd had a tetanus jab last year, when Ali's cat had scratched my arm.

I washed my hand carefully, put antiseptic cream on the bite marks and went back to bed, though I still couldn't sleep. I'd wanted to join Farlan in his twilight fox world and maybe the bite would achieve that. Was I crazy for doing it? Probably. Knowing my luck, I'd get an infection and die alone in the library, slumped over my enormous To Be Read pile.

I sat up suddenly as a terrible thought sprang into my head. Farlan had said that when he'd been bitten, the fox had died. Did that mean Farlan's fox would die? And what about Farlan? Might he die, too? A wave of nausea washed over me at the idea and I dashed into the bathroom so I could splash water on my face. I looked in the grubby mirrored door of the wall cabinet. If I'd killed Farlan by being selfish and unthinking, I'd never forgive myself. I decided to text him. It took me a while to type "Are you OK?" as my hands were trembling. I stared at the phone, willing a response to appear. A few minutes later, my phone pinged.

"Yes. Apart from being woken by a text from a mad woman at 2am"

I sent back an immediate "Sorry".

"Are you OK?" he asked.

"Yes. Sorry. Goodnight from the Mad Woman x"

I laid back and cried with relief.

Chapter 18

The alarm woke me from a deep sleep and I was sluggish at work, though I tried to put on my best smile for the customers. Fiona popped into the shop at lunchtime and seemed pleased with how everything was going. I tried my best to stifle my yawns while she was there. She said takings were up and wastage was down, so my efforts to try and persuade customers to buy older stock were paying dividends.

When I got back to the cottage, I made an early dinner and decided to sit in the library. I picked a book at random from my To Be Read pile. After an hour or so, my eyes began to feel heavy and I woke up, suddenly feeling cold. Except I wasn't in the library anymore. I was standing beneath a hedge, looking across a lawn into a house. I became aware of my surroundings, sniffed the air, pawed the grass beneath me and sensed danger around me. It felt like I was dreaming but I knew it wasn't a dream. I was in a fox's body. I looked admiringly at the russet fur on my paws. I recognised where I was. It was the estate, Farlan's estate. A couple of figures were in view through a pair of French doors and I made a dash to get behind a large stone trough. It was a good vantage point and would afford me protection, in case Shotgun Man was prowling. Farlan strode backwards and forwards looking magnificently fierce. His companion looked as though she was pleading with him. As she drew closer to him, I could see it was Tish. The two of them embraced, she turned her head to rest on his shoulder and smiled. I couldn't see Farlan's face but he didn't pull away, just carried on holding her. My heightened senses inside the fox's body alerted me to movement and I bolted back into the hedge. As I looked from my new hiding place, Farlan turned and smiled. Tish had said to me she and Farlan had a pact to get together if they hadn't married. With him moving to the estate, she would get her wish. They were a perfect couple. It made me sad to think of it but I wasn't sure why; I suppose because I didn't think she wasn't right for him. She was interested in partying and modelling and all manner of bright, shiny things that seemed to me were the opposite of Farlan. But maybe that's who Alex was, making her the ideal Lady to Alex's Laird.

The arrival of the daily text from Farlan woke me just after 10am. I leapt up from the chair in the library and hurriedly showered. By running most of the way, I reached the shop at 10:55am. An artist called Morag was already waiting to get in. I'd seen her a couple of days before. She was staying at the house I'd been in when I first arrived. I'd seen the latest painting she was working on, or at least a photo of it that she'd shown me on her phone. I couldn't help but envy her talent to create beautiful evocations of the landscape. I used to tell people I couldn't draw curtains, but no-one ever seemed to get the joke. My comedic skills matched my artistic ones, it seemed.

Morag followed me into the shop as I opened the door. She wandered around the shelves slowly enough to give me time to get everything switched on and ready.

'OK, Morag. Till's up and running.'

'Thanks, Lucy.' She came straight over and put her basket down next to me so I could swipe the goods through the till.

'I'm having a few people over for drinks and nibbles tonight. Nothing formal. It'll be super if you can come.'

'That's £27.09. Thanks for the invitation. What time?' I had no intention of going. Maybe if Farlan had been around, I would have been more sociable.

'Any time from 6pm. Hard stop at 9pm as I need my beauty sleep, though it's a bit late for that.' She laughed.

She was being modest. She was beautiful, with soft skin that has a translucent quality reminiscent of the sort of marble statues you see in grand museums like the Louvre.

'Though if any hot single men turn up on the ferry, I may end up partying till dawn.' She gave me an exaggerated wink.

'I might see you later, then.' She packed the last of her shopping. I had a feeling she knew I wasn't planning to go.

My phone made a pinging sound. It was a text from Farlan, wondering why I hadn't responded to his earlier message. I lied. "Sorry. Forgot to press send. All OK, though was disturbed by foxy goings on last night."

He sent back a text that said "Sorry". What was he apologising for? That he'd bitten me? Or that I'd seen him and Tish together?

I didn't hang around after shop closing time. I would set my alarm in the morning to give me time to catch up on the shop chores in the morning. I needed to remove the old stock that was at its Use By date. I did take a sorry looking bunch of carrots with me, deciding I'd make soup for my dinner.

I walked quickly back to the cottage but panicked as it came into view. A light was on inside. When I turned the corner, I could see the front door was slightly open. I knew I'd locked it when I left. I had one of those rituals to fix the memory of it in my brain for the day and date. I replayed the memory in my head. Yep, I definitely locked it.

I tiptoed into the main room and could see nothing out of place. Picking up the bread knife from the kitchen, I worked my way as silently as I could along the corridor, tentatively opening each door. There was no-one in my room, the library, the bathroom or the writing room, which just left Farlan's room. In reality it was probably the only room with anything in it worth stealing. I lifted the knife in the air in readiness, pushed open the door noiselessly and a shape came into view from the left. I roared and moved forward then recognised Farlan, barely a moment before the knife was going to make contact with him.

'Fuck!' He sidestepped, knocked the knife from my hand and I fell forward onto the floor. 'Jeez, Lucy, what the fuck are you doing?'

I sat up, rubbing my elbow. 'I thought you were a burglar.' My heart was thumping.

He kicked the knife away.

'Shit, Farlan. You were supposed to call and let me know when you were coming back. A text, something.' I was breathing heavily, mainly from fear.

'Sorry. If I'd realised the price of surprising you was the threat of being stabbed, I would have rung.'

We both took a minute to adjust to the situation as we stared at each other.

I found my voice. 'It's nice to see you. I'm glad I didn't kill you.'

'I'm quite grateful for that, too. Where have you been? Out walking?'

'I've been working.' I was happy that I could finally reveal my secret.

'Working? Where?'

'I'm working in the shop now.'

'In Houbie?'

'I'm on a month's trial.'

'I don't understand. Aren't you supposed to be here on retreat?'

'Let's have a cup of tea. I want to talk to you.'

We walked into the main room.

I filled the kettle and switched it on. 'Have you sorted everything out on the estate now?' I got out two mugs and a spoon.

'All sorted.'

'Good. I do hope you're going to be happy as Laird, I honestly do. So, my big question is whether you'd consider selling this place to me, now you won't be needing it?'

His look of surprise told me I'd misjudged the situation. I thought he'd be delighted that he didn't have to find a buyer. 'Well, if not sell, let me be your tenant for a couple of years. I can't afford an enormous amount but now I'm earning at the shop and getting some cheap food from there as well, I'd hope we can come to some arrangement. I do have some money stashed away from my parents' estate which I promised myself I'd only spend on property. And I'm getting a lump sum from work.'

'Why?' He sounded concerned.

'It turns out there have been redundancies brewing while I've been away. So, I volunteered to leave.' I poured him a mug of tea and we sat down by the unlit fire.

He took a sip, before speaking. 'So, when you're living here, where am I going to be living?'

I frowned. 'Well, on your estate, of course. With Tish.'

When he didn't respond, I carried on talking. 'Let's face it, there was no reason for you to go back to the estate, be away this length of time, unless it was to finalise your move there. If you'd not been interested in doing what your father wanted, you'd have stayed here, wouldn't you?'

'I see. So, I'm being the Laird on the mainland and you've decided you're going to live here permanently?'

'Yes.'

'Alone?'

'Yeah. I mean I've been living here alone while you've been away. I work at the shop most days, get time to read and write and walk, everything you said I should do while I was here. And I love it. I mean, I would like to get a stove and Wi-Fi if I can, but there's Wi-Fi in the café by the shop so it's not a priority. I'd like to give life here a go. I realise it probably sounds a bit crazy, a bit premature to be talking like this, but I feel as though I belong here. That I want to stay here.' It was hard, having to justify my decision.

'Did you read any of the books I left you with?'

'Of course.'

'Did you take anything from them?'

'Tons. I suppose they helped to give me confidence in what my gut was telling me. My Ikigai – my purpose – the what makes me happy. Well, being here is what makes me happy. Using the skills I have – well, the shop work seems to be going OK because of the skills I have. I'm trying to look after myself, eat well and listen to my body, walk most days and be active. I'm using writing as a creative outlet and taking time out to reflect. All these things I'm able to do because I'm here. Though I could do with your expertise when it comes to yoga. It's quite hard to strike a pose when you've a yoga book in one hand.'

'I'll gladly help.'

'As for Kintsugi and Wabi-Sabi, well, I guess it's given me food for thought about accepting who I am, mental scars and all. Being content, mindful, appreciating what I have, finding satisfaction in the small things, counting my blessings – I'm trying to do those things daily. I liked the idea of living life unfiltered and I think it's what being here is all about. It's life stripped to the bare essentials and it's all the more beautiful because of it.' I looked at Farlan. 'Sorry, I'm going on a bit.'

'It's lovely to hear your enthusiasm and hope.'

'I'm trying to think Kaizen, too, though some of the steps I've taken this week have been anything but small.'

'You mean like your job?'

'My job, my home, telling James I'm not going back to him.'

'You've done that too?'

I nodded.

'How did he react?'

'He thinks I'm going through a phase. He's given me till Christmas to come to my senses.'

'I think he's wrong.'

'So do I.'

'And you're sure about all of this?'

'I am. This is absolutely the path I want to follow.'

He stared at me for a while. 'And what if I'm not moving to the mainland?'

Chapter 19

I took a while to process what Farlan was saying. 'I, well, I suppose I'd need to find somewhere else to live, or…but why would you have been away all this time if you weren't moving in there?'

His eyes were dancing with mischief. 'Because I was moving out of there?'

I didn't know what to feel. I was relieved and delighted he wasn't going to be Laird because I was convinced it wouldn't make him happy but I'd got my dream of being here in the cottage on my own, of being mentally and physically self-sufficient and healthy and maybe even a bit wise. That perfect dream was crumbling in front of me, like a sandcastle succumbing to the incoming tide and I ached at its loss. 'Right, so you're staying here then. OK. Well, that's great. I'm pleased.'

'Are you?'

'I'm pleased for you because I think being Farlan suits you much better than being Alex. Even though Alex was a much sharper dresser.'

He looked down at his clothes and laughed. 'That is certainly true. But your dream. I've shot it down.'

'Don't worry about that.'

'I hope you know you're welcome to stay here as long as you like.'

'That's kind of you, but I couldn't impose myself on you long-term, that wouldn't be fair. It's all very well you offering me a room in your retreat while I sort my head out, but I want to give living on the island a proper go. And if you and Tish are spending time here, you'd want privacy.'

He began to laugh and carried on laughing till tears started to run down his cheeks. 'Can you imagine Tish setting foot in this place?'

I suppose it did seem a bit ridiculous.

'Why the hell do you think Tish and I would be spending time together?'

'I saw you. You and her. Canoodling in the drawing room, with the moonlight streaming in.'

'What you actually saw was her canoodling, as you call it, and me resisting her advances. She kept reminding me about our teenage pact to marry. I tried to let her down as gently as I could but she wouldn't take a subtle hint. I had to be pretty blunt in the end and tell her I didn't love her. She didn't take it well and I had to comfort her.'

'Poor her. She seemed very keen on you. Why did you decide not to become Laird?'

He smiled at me. 'Apart from the fact that I'd hate it? Because, as I suspected, Pa has run the estate into the ground. He's been using his capital to fund his lifestyle over the last few years and there's not much of that money left.'

'And when it gets sold and they divide the proceeds amongst the rest of them?'

'I don't think there'll be a lot to go around.'

'That's sad. Not for them but for you. That it'll no longer be in your family.'

'My father bought the estate. It's not as though it's been ours for generations.'

'But all the portraits of your ancestors, up the stairs?'

'They're real enough but not in that setting. There was a smaller house and estate, about twenty miles up the road, till Pa decided to upsize.'

'You seem quite pleased about it all.'

'Do I? That's not very nice of me, is it?'

'It's understandable, given your difficult relationship with your father.'

He gave me the loveliest smile. 'You always give people the benefit of the doubt, don't you? You look for the best in them, try and put the most positive spin on their behaviour.'

'James used to say I was irritatingly nice. He'd call me a soft touch who'd let everyone walk all over me because I only saw the good in them.'

'Well, that goes to show what a dickhead he is, doesn't it?' Farlan looked at me pointedly.

I opened my mouth on auto-pilot, about to defend the alternate point of view, then stopped. 'Yeah, he is a dickhead.'

Farlan's deep-throated laugh made me smile. 'Good for you, Lucy. Not such a soft touch after all.'

'Mainly thanks to your advice. So, you're coming back to carry on the retreat? Keep helping out lost souls like me?'

'I think so. I'm finally starting to be at peace with the world, now the black cloud of my father's expectation isn't hanging over me. I want to keep giving something back and use my skills to help people. Father did, it turned out, leave me some oil paintings. The proceeds from their sale should keep me going here for a few years. I'm also hoping I can get another person involved in running the retreat with me.'

I wondered if he'd already got a friend in mind, a fellow psychiatrist or some other type that specialised in mental health. Not that there was any room for another person in the cottage. Though if his doctor friend was a woman, someone he liked, there'd be no need for an extra bed. I sighed and bit my lip.

He took my empty mug. 'Do you fancy going out for a walk? I know it's getting dark but it'll be good to go and look out from the cliffs. I think the view will be worth it.'

I wasn't sure why the view would be worth it at night, but I went along with it. I was still feeling a bit down-hearted from the loss of my dream of cottage living but I had to believe something would turn up. I couldn't have come all this way only to end up leaving.

We walked to Funzie and beyond to the cliffs where the seals lived, mostly walking without words. We stood, listening to the waves crashing and splashing below us, with occasional moonlight providing enough illumination to make out the white tips. As we stood there, Farlan seemed to be waiting for something.

I looked at him as he stared out to sea, feeling a whirl of emotions towards him.

'Look!' he said.

I followed his gaze and the sky began to burst into light. 'Oh, wow!' was all I could think to say. I had never seen the Northern

Lights before and I stood, mouth open, as the sky danced and paraded its beauty above me.

Farlan spoke softly as I stared in wonderment. 'You asked me about the hanging incident. It wasn't revenge. No-one was hanged. Someone tried to hang themselves.'

I brought myself back from the sky and considered his words. As I thought about what Mrs Mac had said, the truth dawned on me. 'Oh, shit. You tried to hang yourself after the punishment at school.' A ball of sadness lodged inside me at the thought of the little boy who had no choice but to try and end his life.

He nodded. 'It started as soon as I got to the school. The bigger boys picked on the smaller ones, that was tradition but because my mother was dead, they seemed to delight in teasing me about my heritage. They said I was a bastard, that my father was a gamekeeper. I put up with that. But then this one boy, McMahon, started saying my mother had been a loose woman who'd screwed half the men in the area and I could be anyone's child. I could cope with them saying horrible things about me but not about her. When McMahon said it and hit me, I hit him back. He went to the headmaster and I was punished. And the head said I had to apologise to McMahon for hitting him. I refused. I told the headmaster McMahon deserved it and he continued to punish me until I apologised. I wouldn't back down. After a couple of weeks, the head took it on as a personal crusade, to get me to apologise but I wouldn't let him or McMahon win. Had I known McMahon was his second cousin, I might have realised the head would take it on himself to break me. He couldn't have boys fighting back against the regime, the hierarchy. It was what the school was built on.'

'Did you tell your father any of this?'

'I tried but he wasn't interested. Said I was being a sneak and I had to find a way to deal with it myself. I kept defying the head and he kept on punishing me, more and more, harder and harder.'

Tears were forming in my eyes at the story.

'I decided I'd rather die than carry on or give in. Of course, I don't think, aged nine, I comprehended the idea of death and suicide but I had to break the cycle. I couldn't think of any other way to get my father to realise I wasn't going back to that school. Father went there before me, you see. He'd put up with the punishment, too. He'd been picked on. He'd held out for a few weeks before apologising to his appointed bully and said it had been the making of him, to understand his place in the world. He thought I should be broken too. He was too inflexible to see I was different from him and would never sully my mother's name in front of a person like McMahon. Father refused to listen to my pleas. He kept saying it was for my own good.'

'But he must have listened after you did what you did?'

'I gave him no choice, did I? He could hardly send me back after that. But he never forgave me for it.'

'Was it your father who found you?'

'No. I did it in one of the outbuildings. One of the estate workers saw me on the way home from work and cut me down. Just in time, according to the doctor.'

'And you were allowed to change school?'

'I was sent to the local school. The kids hated me there for coming from the posh house and once they saw me get undressed for games, they were pretty horrible to me about the scars on my body. In comparison though, it was bliss. Father took every opportunity after that to try and make me be what he wanted me to be, someone in his own image, but it never worked. Not even with this latest stunt from beyond the grave.'

'Thank you for telling me. I appreciate your honesty.' I squeezed his hand but instantly regretted it, wincing from my wounds.

'Sorry. I tried to bite as gently as I could. Why did you want me to do it?'

'Curiosity? Jealousy? Are you still having your foxy jaunts? Or has that passed to me?'

'I am, so I'm hoping our foxes might be able to go on jaunts together. Why did you text me that night?'

'I was worried your fox would die and then I panicked that you might die as well.'

'And when that didn't finish me off, you thought you'd try with the bread knife?'

I gave him a sideways look.

'Just joking.' He his gaze back to the sea.

I turned back to look at the horizon and listened to the waves as I waited with him.

As the sky began to dance again, he stepped forward and turned to face me. 'I've known since I left school that I wanted a simple way to live and it's taken me a long time to find it. But it still wasn't enough. With everything that's happened lately, I finally worked out what was missing, why being here on the island hadn't fulfilled me in the way I thought it would. It was because I needed someone with me, someone who will love the simple life, who'll thrive in this environment. Who loves the island and is empathetic enough to work with me at the retreat.' He continued to gaze at me. 'I've often wondered what it would be like to find someone who is special enough to fill the gap in my life, who feels like my soulmate. Someone who it feels is so right for you, whose company you crave and who makes you feel so happy that your heart might burst.'

How could I tell him I didn't need to wonder because he'd described my feelings for him. I'd not dared articulate it even to myself but I knew I was besotted with him. I'd even got his fox to bite me as a way of getting closer to him. I dropped my gaze as my breath shortened and my heart thumped in my chest but I didn't dare speak, so I waited to see what he would say or do next.

He lifted my chin with his fingertips so I was looking at him. His fox's eyes sparkled at me, brighter than I'd ever seen them before with the lights in the sky reflecting off them. I wondered if mine looked the same to him.

'It's you, Lucy. It's you. I had to go away from here to see if my feelings were real, but I missed you so much, as much as I missed the island. I was afraid you'd have left when I got back, but I had to give you the chance to go home before I dared tell you how I feel.' He looked at me, searching my expression for a response to his declaration.

'I've been trying not to think of you this way, Farlan. When James suggested I'd fallen for someone up here, I knew it was true. I knew I wanted to be with you. But I didn't dare think about it, in case I was just another visitor to the retreat who you'd expect to leave, like Jenna and all the others did.' I looked at him and smiled.

He pulled me towards him and kissed me, softly at first but more urgently as I responded to his passion.

I opened my eyes and pulled away. 'Are you sure you want me? A brandy-guzzling, chocolate-chomping lazy bum with enormous thighs?'

'Hey, I'm not saying there couldn't be some improvements.' He gave that lovely laugh of his.

'I'll do my best to be better.'

'Hey, I'm a whisky-guzzling, porridge-slurping fool, who's given up a vast estate and a lucrative medical career to live in a shack at the end of the world. I'd say you're getting the worst deal here.'

'But you do have a lovely body to compensate.'

'Oh, Lucy. I can't believe you want this life. When you said you'd got a job here, I dared to believe you might want to stay here with me.'

'It's the first job I've had where I feel at home. And I think I'm good at it. Chatting to people, helping them, making sure things don't go to waste, being a part of the community. It's not exactly making the most of all my skills, the lucrative ones, but it's focused on the skills that are important to me.'

He put his hand against my cheek. 'It's good to hear you talking positively about yourself.'

I shivered with excitement and cold.

'Let's get back home.'

We walked hand-in-hand to the cottage and I could feel my heart beating in my ears from the anticipation of a future in this world that a few weeks before I'd not known. The sky continued dancing but not as much as my heart.

I told him about Morag's party so we stopped in on the way back. The party had gone on much later than she'd planned. I couldn't see any hot new men among the partygoers, but Morag was dancing away with Fiona and Rory, happily missing out on her beauty sleep. Farlan held my hand as we walked around and he introduced me to some islanders I'd not yet met. There were some nudges when the locals who knew him spotted the intimacy between us but people seemed happy about it. We stayed for one drink before our desire to be alone overtook us.

Fiona pulled me to one side as we were leaving. 'I've not seen Farlan look this happy before. Or you.'

I hugged her. 'Thank you. I don't think I've ever felt as happy as I do now.'

And I knew, as I laid with Farlan in his bed, that a life being bathed in his love, living in the fresh, wild air of Fetlar with endless time to read and write, was what I wanted, more than any other life.

And while Farlan and I slept, holding on to each other as if our lives depended on it, our fox selves began to frolic together in the cottage's garden, away from prying eyes, safe in the shadows of our earthly world.

Farlan's fox had at last lost the need to stray from home in search of his destiny. And my fox had no desire to be anywhere but here.

Dear Reader

Thank you for buying *Son of the Furrows*.

If you enjoyed the world of Lucy and Farlan, it would be great if you could put a rating or review on Amazon or Goodreads. If you're new to my work, you may enjoy some of my other books, which you can buy from your local Amazon site.

Jane Sleight

Novels

The *Tales of a Modern Woman* trilogy

Part 1 - Teen Rebel to Woman

Part 2 – From Woman to Wife

Part 3 – Happy Ever After?

Standalone Novels

Sasha

Faking It

Novellas

Walking Back Toward Myself

Like Father, Like Son

The Secret of Contentment

Short Stories and Poetry

Crumbs from the Bread of Life

Printed in Great Britain
by Amazon